WICKED
OATH

DEMONS AFTER DARK  COVENANT

JENNA WOLFHART

Wicked Oath

Book Three of Demons After Dark: Covenant

Copyright © 2021 by Jenna Wolfhart

Cover Art by Covers by Juan

❀ Created with Vellum

"Welcome to Hell."

I gazed up at the demon city sprawled across the looming hillside. An ancient, crumbling wall wrapped around clusters of buildings built from brushed black stone. Flames licked the parched ground, and thick shadows whorled through the night sky.

It was kind of creepy, but it definitely wasn't the nightmare hellscape I'd been expecting.

Where were the screams of pain? Where were the tortured human souls boiling for eternity?

Minus the tiny fires and the weird shadows, the city looked pretty normal. Old. But normal.

I glared up at Lucifer, his expression hooded and impossible to read. He'd barely spoken to me during our entire week-long trek through the underworld's fiery deserts. Zero of my million questions had been answered. About three days in, I'd given up trying to get anything out of him. Temporarily. I wouldn't be silenced for long.

"So, this is it, huh? Kind of disappointing."

Lucifer shot me a smile full of teeth, flashing like the silver hair that curled around his ears. "Only you would find Allyria disappointing."

I shrugged. "Where are the hellbeasts and the mountains of flames? Those little fires around the wall don't exactly inspire terror."

Something odd flickered in the depths of his eyes, but it vanished too quickly for me to read it. "Allyria is my home. The soul torture happens elsewhere."

I fought back a shudder at his complete lack of empathy. The last thing I wanted to do was let him see just how freaked out I was about this whole thing. But on a scale of one to ten, I was a level thirteen at the bare minimum.

I'd been through a few shitty situations in my life, but this was by far the worst. I mean, let's be honest. There wasn't even any competition. The actual King of Hell had abducted me and taken me into the underworld. It couldn't get much worse than that.

I hoped.

Lucifer had refused to tell me what he'd done to Az and the rest of the Legion. I tried not to imagine the worst—that he'd destroyed them all and hidden their hearts across the furthest corners of the earth. At least I knew Serena and Priyanka were safe, even if they were probably totally freaked out. Hopefully, they wouldn't find the hellgate and follow us here.

Even though I hadn't seen any of the hellbeasts yet, I knew they were out there. Somewhere. They might even be watching me.

"Come along." Lucifer gripped my elbow and jerked

me forward. "Enough chitchat. Time to introduce you to your new home."

I rolled my eyes but went along with it. If he truly thought he could trap me here for eternity, he had another think coming. The second he let down his guard, I'd find a way to escape. Maybe it would take a month or a year. But one day, he would make a mistake.

He might be the King of Hell, but he wasn't all-knowing. That much I was sure of.

Lucifer dragged me to a swirling wrought-iron gate that was at least five times taller than I was. Two soldiers stood on either side, decked in steel armor that looked a lot like what human soldiers wore back in the Middle Ages. Crimson feathers sprouted from their helms, and only their glowing eyes were visible. Weird.

"Your Highness." The soldiers spoke in unison as they bowed before their king.

"Open the gates," Lucifer replied in a lazy drawl. "Unagi."

I cocked my head and fought back a laugh. "Unagi? What's that all about?"

"None of your concern," Lucifer said tightly as the guards rushed to open the gates. The iron groaned as they dragged it open, the burnt sand puffing up in its wake. Lucifer tightened his grip on my elbow and jerked me through without another word to the guards.

The winding streets of Allyria were quiet and dark, and the scent of fire burned through the night air. I glanced down at the cobblestones beneath my black boots and noted a few stables and neighing horses down some alleys we passed. There were no streetlamps or electric wires. No blue glow of televisions. It was like we were stuck in the past. The *human* past.

3

And everything was deathly quiet. We didn't pass a single other demon on our trek up the hill to the massive structure that loomed over everything else.

As I gazed around, I realized the true nature of this place. The way the paths wound together, forming an intricate design in the very center. The city had been built in the pattern of Lucifer's seal.

Okay, so maybe Allyria was creepier than it looked.

"This is the Temple of Solomon," Lucifer murmured as he led me through a tall archway that tunnelled into the depths of the structure. I didn't really know what to call the building. It wasn't a castle or anything like that, but it also looked nothing like a modern home back in the human world. It rose high into the air, built from smooth black stone. There were no doors. Only archways. And not a single window held glass, not even on the highest floors.

"A temple," I muttered. "So that everyone can worship you, I'm guessing. What a narcissist."

"I find it intriguing that you're so eager to insult your captor, who also happens to be the most powerful demon in the world."

"You've just proven my point by calling yourself the most powerful demon in the world. Your ego is unparalleled."

"It isn't ego, Mia, when it's an objective truth."

I rolled my eyes. "Sure thing, Mr. Big Daddy Demon. If you're so powerful, why are you so scared to let me run free?"

He stiffened, grinding his teeth. Aha. So, I was right then. I'd spent a lot of time deep in thought during our week-long trek through the underworld's desert wastes. And I'd come to one very important conclusion.

Something about me terrified Lucifer. I posed some kind of threat. If not directly to him, then to his soul game. Why else would he be so laser-focused on keeping me away from Asmodeus? Why else would he have dragged me here?

He'd wiped my memories. He'd hidden me from Az. And now he'd stolen me away to the underworld. The only thing I couldn't understand was why he hadn't just killed me again. Seemed a lot easier than all the scheming he'd done.

"That memory box didn't work exactly how I expected," he finally muttered.

Frowning, I glanced up at him. The chandelier light glimmered against his silver hair. "What do you mean?"

"I mean exactly what I said. You remember so little."

Something in the tone of his voice made my heart flip. Unease twisted my gut, turning my mouth into the parched desert outside these city walls. "I remember Az. That's all I need to know."

But that was a lie, and we both knew it. As terrifying as it all was, I was desperate to understand what the hell was going on here. Whatever Lucifer's motives were, there wasn't a single doubt in my mind that it had something to do with my past life as a fallen angel. It all tied together. Somehow. And I would never figure out how to beat him if I didn't have all the information.

I'd never find a way to get back to Az. Wherever he was.

Our footsteps echoed off the looming stone walls as Lucifer led me down a silent corridor. A stairwell rose up at the end, spiralling up into darkness. I glanced around, searching for any hint as to what went on here. Other than the obvious demon worshipping, of course.

"Why's it so quiet?" I jumped at the echoing bounce of my own voice. *Quiet, quiet, quiet* repeated in my ear like something straight out of a horror movie.

Lucifer continued striding purposefully down the hallway toward the creepy stairs.

"It's the middle of the night," he said with a slight smile, clearly basking in my growing sense of unease. "Everyone is sleeping."

"Right." It was still weird to think that demons actually slept. Immortal beings who tortured souls and probably feasted on bones. Okay, so Az didn't do that and neither did the others in his Legion. But I wouldn't put it past Lucifer.

"You'll meet them in the morning."

My brows winged upward. "Is that really necessary? Aren't you just going to toss me into a dungeon cell or something?"

As far as I was aware, Lucifer had given up on the whole bride thing. He'd flat out said he didn't want to marry me. Because I annoyed him. Thankfully. For the love of god, surely he hadn't changed his mind.

If he had, I'd have to do something annoying to remind him. Maybe kick him in his balls? That ought to go over well.

He chuckled. "No dungeon cell. That's hardly necessary, given your condition."

I scrunched my nose, frowning. "My condition? What the hell is that supposed to mean?"

He came to a sudden stop and whirled on me. When he leaned forward to sneer into my face, he brought the scent of fire along with him. "You may have once posed a threat to me, back in a different life. But you're mortal now. There's nothing you can do to harm me or anyone who calls Hell their home."

I fought back the urge to snarl into his face. He wanted to get under my skin. He wanted to piss me off so he could savor my anger. I wouldn't give him the satisfaction.

"It's odd, isn't it?" I asked in a calm, steady voice. There wasn't even a hint of fear in my words. Take that, Mr. Big Daddy Demon.

He cocked his head. "*What* is odd?"

"Your reaction to me." I smiled. "There's something behind it. Something you're hiding. I might not know what it is now, Lucifer, but I will one day. I'll find out what you don't want me to know, and I'll finally do the very thing you fear."

Obviously, I was just talking out of my ass. But I wanted to rattle him. He wanted to see me squirm? *Ha!* I'd make him squirm instead. Two could play his twisted game.

"Nice try." He leaned forward and tapped my forehead with two fingers, his hand in the shape of a gun. "Even if you manage to unlock your fucked up mind, you're still mortal, Mia McNally. I killed you once, when you were a powerful immortal being. Test me too many times, and I'll have to kill you again. In fact, I will *relish* in it."

My heart pounded, and I quickly glanced away so that he couldn't see the fear in my eyes. Though I knew he could smell it. Damn demons.

"Whatever," I muttered, at a loss for a good come-back this time. Seemed the fear of death yanked all the logical thoughts out of my brain. Who would have thought, right?

We reached the stairwell, and Lucifer led me through the thickening shadows. Up and up and up we went. There were no lightbulbs here. Not even a flickering torch to light the way.

Just Lucifer, glowering in the darkness.

When we reached the top of the stairs, Lucifer hung a left down another dark hallway. With the brushed black stone, everything looked exactly the same, giving me the sinking feeling that he was leading me through a maze. One intended to trap me for the rest of my mortal life.

He stopped outside an actual door, one of the few I'd seen since walking into the Temple of Solomon. It led into a sparsely-decorated bedroom with nothing more than a twin bed and a wall of empty bookshelves.

"Wow, this is cozy," I said, rolling my eyes at Lucifer's back as he strode over to the window that looked out onto the dark, sprawling city. A light breeze ruffled my hair—still brown from the fae's glamor. There wasn't a single pane of glass protecting me from the elements, and if I had wings, it'd be an easy way out. Unfortunately for me, I hadn't inherited feathers from my former self.

"I thought you'd like it," he said quietly. "You've stayed in this room before."

I blinked. "Wait, what?"

Surely he was fucking with me.

He sighed. "You heard me."

"I think it's time you explained things to me." I folded my arms and glared at his shadowy silhouette by the window. All I could see was the swirling tattoo that spread across the back of his neck and down the length of his left arm. "You wanted me to find that memory box and use it. And you thought it would make me

8

remember everything. Which meant you *wanted* me to remember. So, why all the secrecy now? Why not just tell me what you want with me?"

My voice had slowly risen during my little speech until it practically boomed all around us. Anger rushed through my veins, transforming my hands into shaking fists. I hated him. With every fiber of my being. And I couldn't let him win.

With a deep breath, I turned my gaze onto the window. The very large window with zero glass. We were so far above the ground...maybe I could push him out and run.

It was a crazy idea. Or was it?

I wet my lips as my heartbeat picked up speed. Fear and anger tumbled through my gut, but that wouldn't give my thoughts away. My emotions weren't any different than they had been five minutes before. He'd never see it coming. I didn't even need to push him that hard. Just a little shove.

I couldn't really do this. Right? Lucifer was the King of Hell. He was far more powerful than me, even when I'd been a fallen angel.

He had wings. If I pushed him, would he even fall?

If I caught him off guard, he might not have time to open his wings. He'd tumble toward the ground. And go splat. Like a bug.

This was crazy.

My heart rattled in my chest. Desperation clogged my throat, drowning me in it.

I had to try. It might be the only way out of this.

Blinking back my angry tears, I rushed toward him with a speed I didn't know I had. With a roar, I shoved his back as hard as I could. He stumbled forward. His foot twisted beneath him, and he hurtled out the window.

My fingers flew to my lips.

With my heart in my throat, I whirled on my feet and ran.

2

My boots pounded the sleek stone floor. Arms windmilling, I flew down the stairs and rushed out into the darkness. The scent of fire peppered the air, but it was the sweetest thing I'd ever smelled. It was the scent of freedom.

I whirled toward the street leading out of the city. Thank the gods it was the middle of the night. I could sneak out of here without any demon residents or hell-beasts spotting me before I escaped. I tried not to think about the guards at the gate and the long trek through the desert that would come after. I'd deal with that when I got there.

First up, get the hell out of Allyria.

Sucking in a desperate breath, I hurtled forward with the speed of someone trying to flee from a horde of zombies. Hell, I'd happily take zombies over my current situation. Not the bastards from *Resident Evil*. The classic kind that just lumbered around moaning. They might try to eat my brains, but at least I could outrun them.

I flew to the left, retracing the steps we'd taken to get to the Temple of Solomon.

Suddenly, Lucifer thundered down right in my path, his midnight wings flared wide on either side of his body. Ash swirled from his skin, his tattoo writhing like dozens of hungry snakes.

I swallowed hard and stumbled back. That was...new.

His eyes flashed as he stalked toward me. "You tried to kill me."

"No, I didn't. I knew you wouldn't die if I pushed you out of the window. I'm not an idiot." I cast a glance around the maze of streets, searching for an escape route. But anything I tried now would fail. He knew this city far better than I did. And he had demonic speed on his side. "I was, however, hoping it would knock you unconscious."

He flashed me a wicked smile. "You'll have to try harder than that."

"Maybe I will."

"You know what I think, Mia?" His wings furled and vanished into his back. "I think you talk a big game, but you're far more afraid of me than you want to admit."

I rolled my eyes, hoping he couldn't hear the frantic patter of my heart. "I just want to go back home. It has nothing to do with fear."

It had a hell of a lot to do with fear.

He swept his gaze across me, cocking his head. "You really are *nothing* like I expected."

My spidey senses tingled. He'd said this once before, and he'd hinted at it on several other occasions. There was something big he wasn't telling me, and I was sick and tired of being in the dark.

I folded my arms. "Listen, I know you want to be the big, bad secretive demon, but that's going to get you nowhere with me. I'm going to keep doing things like this unless you tell me exactly what is going on. What do you want from me? What have you done with Az? Where is the Legion? Tell me now, Lucifer, or I will make your life a living hell."

Lucifer chuckled and mimicked my stance. Arms folded, chin lifted, eyes narrowed and full of fire. It was like looking into a mirror. If that mirror held an image of a massive, muscular demon with ash flowing off his skin.

"You do realize that I'm the King of Hell, right? I don't have to tell you a goddamn thing."

"Well, then have fun falling out of a window the next time I catch you off guard."

He sneered. "Please. Don't be ridiculous. You don't really think a weak mortal girl can catch *me* off guard, do you?"

I smiled. "I already did it once."

Ash sprayed into my face, stinging my skin. Lucifer stepped closer and stared at me for a good, long while, his expression unreadable. Thoughts were swirling around in his head, but I couldn't begin to imagine what they were. Had I pushed him too far? Did I even care? He clearly wanted me alive. What was the worst that could happen?

Chuckling, he stepped in close and wrapped his hand around my elbow, jerking me toward the Temple. "You have no idea how close I am to throwing you in with the wolves and watching them rip you to shreds."

I shuddered as he dragged me down the street. "Nice try. If you haven't killed me by now, you won't."

He cut me a sideways glance. "You're right. There's something I need from you first."

A chill swept down my spine, and I swallowed down a lump in my throat. This was exactly what I wanted, but his tone of voice put me on edge. It sounded like the sharp edge of a sword. "Well then. You've certainly changed your tune quickly."

"You're annoying me, and while there's nothing you can do to threaten me, I don't have the patience to deal with your constant escape attempts. I have far more important things to focus on than trying to guess what you're plotting behind my back."

"Not really *behind* your back. I think I've been pretty blunt about how much I despise you."

Lucifer was silent for the rest of the return trek to the Temple. I couldn't get anything more out of him, no matter how much I peppered him with questions. Annoying really. Why tell someone you wanted something from them and not say what it was?

After he led me back into the building, he jerked me through a doorway that opened up into a massive library. It was at least five stories tall, lined by rows upon rows of beautiful, leather-bound books. Their spines shimmered beneath the dim glow of the candle-light scattered throughout the expansive space.

My brows rocketed up to my hairline. "A library in the depths of Hell? Seems flammable."

"Fire doesn't penetrate the black stone," he muttered as he strode to the center of the room and leaned against a long oak table. A chandelier hung above it, suspended in the air without any ropes or chains.

"Might want to rethink all those candles then."

"Those aren't real flames." He sighed and ran a hand

down his face before resting his fingers against the swirling tattoo on his neck. "Mia, you and I both know I've brought you here for a reason."

I perked up a bit, straightening. "And you're finally going to tell me why."

A strange smile lifted the corners of his lips. "I was going to let you settle into your room and have a good night's sleep in a comfortable bed after the long week of camping we just had. But I can see now that's not going to work."

I barked out a laugh. "Settle in? You've got to be kidding me. This is Hell, not some five-star resort with a spa and room service."

"You'd be surprised," he murmured.

"No, I wouldn't."

"I have a deal to offer you."

My heart flipped, and I stumbled back. "Oh god. No. Not this again. I've had it with you demons and your deals."

He cocked his head, frowning. "You haven't even heard the terms yet."

"I don't need to." I took a step back toward the door. Time to attempt another hasty escape. "I've heard enough. I said this to Az, and I'll say it to you, too. I'm never signing another demon contract. My soul is mine, and I'll never risk losing it again."

"Hmm." His hands gripped the edge of the table, and I swore I heard a loud snap. Yikes. "You'll change your mind when you hear what I have to say."

"Nope." I let out a bitter laugh. "Absolutely not."

"You're wrong."

"You'll let me return to the real world, right?" I

shook my head and took another step toward the door. "Nope. You'll have to do better than that."

"Oh, I will." He pushed away from the table and stalked toward me. "This isn't about you, Mia. It's about the entire world. Sign my contract, and you'll save them all."

Say what now?

"The entire world," I repeated dumbly.

"Yes. You can save the world if you agree to my deal."

The blood rushed out of my cheeks. All I could do was stare up into his cruel face, the heavy thump of my heart echoing in my ears. His eyes were hooded and closed off, but the tension in his shoulders was barely there. He didn't look like someone who had just threatened the future existence of the world for a fucking demon deal.

Lucifer was a goddamn sociopath.

"I don't think I understand," I finally answered, still trying to decide if I'd hallucinated this entire thing. It didn't make any sense. Maybe he was right, and I needed some sleep.

"It's simple, really, Mia." His smile stretched wide. "I need you to do something for me. In return, I will stop the game of souls."

My mouth dropped open. I snapped it shut, but then dropped it open a second time. Now, I really *was* hallucinating. Lucifer and the Creator had been playing the game of souls for...centuries. They were both getting close to a win, based on some very dodgy math I'd done in my head a few weeks ago. So, why give in now? For...my soul?

I shook my head. "Stop fucking with me. Is this some

kind of twisted demon torture or something? Are you just doing this because I pushed you out of a window? I think we've both established that it didn't hurt you. So you can stop this weird game. You catching me is enough of a punishment."

"I have never been more serious in my life, Mia."

I stared up into his face. The cruel anger had vanished, replaced by something more akin to hopeful need. Furrowing my brows, I tried to understand. What could Lucifer possibly need from me that would make him stop his game? I was just a human. Reincarnated from a fallen angel but still. It wasn't like I had any powers.

I sucked in a breath of hope. "You would stop the game? Just like that?"

"Just like that." He nodded. "If you do what I ask."

"What about the other side? The angels. They'd agree to end the game?"

"There's a clause. Iron-clad. I drew up the contract myself. If either side forfeits, the game ends without a winner." He shrugged. "It's just that neither side has ever been willing to give in."

"So, the soul game would just stop. The world wouldn't go to Heaven *or* Hell."

"That's right."

I narrowed my eyes. "I find this really hard to believe. There has to be a catch."

"There is." His dark gaze shuttered over that strange, unexpected hope. "You're not going to like what I ask you to do. It might shatter you."

Chills swept along my bare arms. "Just tell me. I'm stronger than you think."

"It's not about strength." He turned away, striding

back to the table. Hands fisted by his sides, he kept his gaze away from me. "I need you to destroy Asmodeus. You have to rip out his heart."

My blood roared in my ears. I waited for the punch-line or the cruel laugh at my expense. He really was just fucking with me now. He wanted to get back at me for pushing him out of a window, and so here we were. Asshole.

But the laugh never came.

"Come on," I said, my voice echoing through the lofted, silent room. "I know this is a joke, Lucifer."

"It's not a joke." He kept his back turned my way.

"Yeah, right. You expect me to believe that the King of Hell wants a mortal girl to rip out her demon lover's heart?"

"You may not want to believe it, but it's the truth." He finally turned back toward me, his gaze dark. "Kill him, and I'll end the game of souls."

I blinked at him. This was the most bizarre moment of my life. And here I'd thought being dragged through a hellgate had been the weirdest so far.

"So, you're seriously telling me that you will end the game of souls you've been playing *for centuries* if I give you Az's heart?" I levelled my gaze. "That's what you're actually telling me right now."

He nodded.

I barked out a laugh. "I mean, no. My answer is no. Surely you didn't think I'd agree to something like that."

His sharp gaze pierced right through me. "Think about what you're turning down, Mia."

"I don't need to think about it. I know my answer. And it's no."

"All those souls," he said, stepping toward me. "So

many saved. The world would continue to go on, just as it is."

I shivered. "I'm not going to kill Az, Lucifer."

"You're willing to sacrifice thousands of lives for his?"

Blood rushed through my head. Wincing, I turned away, hating the angry tears that filled my eyes. I did not want Lucifer to see me cry.

"It's not as simple as that, and you know it." My words came out gargled.

"You're right. I do know it's not that simple. Just as you know you shouldn't dismiss my deal so easily. Think of all the lives you'd save, Mia."

"Stop it." I squeezed my eyes tight. "Why would you even do this? If you want Az dead, why would you want *me* to do it?"

Why wouldn't he just do it himself? He was the actual devil. The most powerful demon in the world as he himself had so boldly stated. It would make far more sense for him to do it, but I kept those thoughts to myself. Didn't want to give him any ideas.

"Because it's the only way to ensure he doesn't reunite with you when he comes back."

I flipped opened my eyes, zeroing in on his words. "Come back? You mean reincarnation, don't you? Like what happened to me." Fisting my hands, I stalked toward Lucifer. "What is all this about? It has something to do with what happened before, Az and me, and—"

"I think that's enough for tonight," he cut in sharply.

Throwing up my hands, I growled at him. "You can't just drop a bomb like that and then not expect me to ask any questions. You're going to tell me exactly—"

"I can do whatever I like," he hissed, grabbing my

elbow and yanking me toward the door. "This conversation is over, and it's time for you to go to your room. Attempt to escape all night if you wish, but I must warn you, there will be guards assigned to you. Ones you will not wish to meet."

3

Somehow, my life had led me here. I was a prisoner in Hell, being offered the chance to save the world. As long as I murdered my boyfriend.

Was he my boyfriend? Hell if I even knew at this point. It wasn't like we'd put words to our connection. I'd never really had the chance to tell him how I felt...which was a lot of things. I didn't want to use the big L word. Not yet. In my past life, I'd been madly, deeply in love with him. But that was a different Mia.

That girl felt like an entirely different person, even though she was me. Even though our souls were somehow the same. I still felt like my own damn self. I wasn't *really* her. And yet, that connection with Asmodeus had remained.

It had always been there, even when I'd hated his guts.

Lucifer was delirious to think I'd ever do anything to hurt him. Much less erase his existence from the world.

Still...the demon king's words replayed in my mind as I tried to find sleep. He was willing to give up the game. So many lives saved. So many souls free from eternal torment.

How could he be *that* motivated to see Az die?

It didn't make any sense.

The next morning came far too quickly. Even in Hell, the sun rose high in the sky, blanketing the city in pink and orange light. I groaned and threw the sheets back from the bed before padding over to the window. Staring down at the ground, I wished I had wings. Lucifer knew exactly what he was doing by keeping me in a room without glass. There was a way out of here, and it was achingly close. But I couldn't use it.

The day slowly passed without any sign of Lucifer or the demons that inhabited the Temple. I spent most of my time gazing out the window to get a glimpse of the city's residents, but the streets were too far away for me to make out much. I spotted a flash of movement a few times but nothing more than that. Probably for the best. These demons were nothing like Az.

Time passed, and the sky darkened. That was when the knock on the door finally came.

No one waited for me to open it. It swung wide, revealing Lucifer dressed in loose black pants and a button-up shirt that hung open from his bellybutton up. His muscular chest gleamed in the moonlight along with the silver hair hanging into his piercing eyes.

"Go away. The answer is still no." I crossed my arms and shot him a glare.

He smiled. "A pity. I thought you would have liked to have some food."

My stomach growled, betraying me. "So now you're not going to feed me unless I do what you demand? I've got to sign a contract just to eat?"

Breakfast and lunch had never come. Not even a glass of water. I was parched.

"No need." He opened the door wider and motioned me to join him in the hallway. "You will come have dinner with me."

Hmm. "What's the catch?"

"There is no catch, Mia. You need to eat."

I narrowed my eyes. "If you think I need to eat, then what happened to lunch and breakfast?"

"My apologies," he said smoothly. "I simply forgot. It's been a very long time since I've had a mortal guest, and we don't need to eat quite as regularly as you do."

"So, you do need to eat," I couldn't help but say. "What happens if you don't?"

He cocked his head. "I'm honestly shocked at how many things you don't remember. What a useless little tool that memory box turned out to be."

I rolled my eyes. "Whatever. I don't want to eat with you."

"You don't have another choice, Mia." His voice turned sharp. "You aren't a guest here. You're my prisoner. And you will come eat with me when I say you will."

Grinding my teeth, I glared at him. "You disgust me."

"I'm not too fond of you either."

"Good," I snapped.

He flashed me his teeth. "Now that we have that sorted, it's time for you to step into this hallway. The sooner you come with me, the sooner we can get this over with."

I huffed. "You know what? Fine."

Lucifer had annoyingly won once again, but the truth

was, I was famished. My mouth practically watered just thinking about the prospect of food. During our journey through the deserts, he'd shared a little bread with me a few times a day, but rarely more than that. If I didn't get some real food in me fast, I wouldn't have the energy to fight back.

Lucifer led me through the black stone maze, past the library, and into a small dining hall where a literal feast sat waiting for us. The entire table was covered in food. Chicken wings, french fries, hamburgers, and pizza. It wasn't at all what I'd been expecting with the whole medieval vibe going on around here, but I wasn't going to be picky. My stomach roared its approval.

Hurriedly, I rushed to the table and plopped into one of the chairs, reaching for the nearest pizza. Cheese, tomato sauce, thin-crust. I'd never needed anything more.

Lucifer took a seat at the far end of the table in front of a plate that held a raw chunk of red meat. The pink of it glistened beneath the chandelier. I paused with my hand halfway to my mouth.

"Don't tell me you're going to eat that."

He picked up his knife and fork. "Don't look so surprised. Mortals eat steak."

"That is not a steak," I said flatly. "That is a raw slab of flesh."

He waved his hand dismissively. "Cooking would ruin it."

"You're an actual animal."

"No, I'm a demon. Just like Asmodeus. You'd do well to remember that."

"Oh, I see what you're doing now." I rolled my eyes and turned back to the pizza. "You want to make me think he's a vicious monster so that I'll do what you want. Well, I've spent a lot of time around him, and I've never seen him chow down on a raw steak."

Lucifer chuckled. "Just because you have never seen Asmodeus do something, doesn't mean he hasn't done it. I would not forget that if I were you, Mia McNally."

Ignoring him, I chomped into the pizza and moaned from the taste of the gooey cheese. Only moments later, I'd stuffed another three slices into my face. I wanted more. I salivated for it. But I'd eaten so little for so many days that my stomach had already begun to cramp.

Stupid demons. Lucifer had somehow managed to ruin a Feast of Junk Food.

A knock sounded on the door as I downed a glass of water. My head jerked to the side to find a tall man striding in, decked out in all black. His eyes were hooded and dark, and fire oozed from his skin. Another demon. My heart picked up speed. He was the first being I'd seen other than Lucifer since I'd arrived.

I'd started to wonder again if they all had horns and tails. Or worse. There had to be some reason they were all so determined to stay out of sight.

"What is it, Pyro?" Lucifer drawled, leaning back in his chair. He looked the part of a king, sitting there like that. The attitude, the strength, the annoying sense of superiority.

I could punch him right in the face.

The demon cut his fiery eyes my way. "Should this wait until you're in a more private environment?"

Lucifer frowned in my direction, pushed up from his chair, and vanished into the hallway with Pyro. I dropped my pizza onto my plate and minced across the floor. If he thought I wasn't going to eavesdrop on this conversation, he was an idiot.

"Tell me what it is, Pyro," Lucifer said in a low voice.

"There's news from Manhattan."

I stood a little straighter. News from Manhattan? Surely that meant Az, right? But why was there news? What had Lucifer done with him? I leaned closer to the door, holding my breath in my throat.

"Go on," Lucifer said.

The demon growled. "Asmodeus and the Legion have started hunting the fallen angels again. They're trying to save souls."

Relief shuddered through me. They were alive. It was the best news I'd ever heard in my life.

"Good. As expected." A beat passed. "Any news from Rafael?"

"Yes. He's searched the river beneath the bridge, but he hasn't managed to find your—"

"That's enough. We have ears."

I stiffened and jumped back from the door but not before Lucifer appeared inside the dining room again. He gave me a slight smile and wandered back over to the table, nonchalant and unbothered. But I'd almost heard something important. I was certain of it. Otherwise, he never would have told Pyro to shut up.

"That was illuminating," I said, following him back over to the table. He settled into his chair and started sawing at his slab of meat. "Or it would have been if you hadn't been lying through your teeth. Don't act like you want Az to save souls because I damn well know you don't."

"Are you going to eat any more of that?" He pointed at my half-eaten pizza. I hadn't even touched the hamburgers and fries, and my churning stomach wouldn't let me.

"I can't believe you're talking about food right now."

"Why ever not? We are sitting at a dinner table, after all. Or at least we were before you decided to listen in on private conversations."

"You know why not." My fisted hands shook by my sides. "First, you offer me a deal to stop your stupid game. Now, you seem to approve of Az saving souls. I really think it's time I know what you're up to, Lucifer."

He laced his hands behind his head and leaned further back in his chair. He looked so calm and collected when I was anything but. Shaking his head, he tsked. "Raising your voice at the dinner table. Such bad manners you mortals have."

I snorted. "Bad manners? You know what's bad manners? Abducting someone and then trying to force her to kill the man she loves."

The word popped out of my mouth before I could stop it. Eyes wide, I clamped a hand over my lips, desperately wishing I could take it back. Obviously, it was just a turn of phrase. Hyperbole. I'd gotten caught up in my emotions, that was all.

And the first time I said that word, I did not want it to be in front of my greatest enemy.

Lucifer arched a brow. As desperately as I wished he'd missed that, of course he hadn't. "Ah, I see. Things make much more sense now. I didn't get to you quickly enough."

"Stop talking in riddles."

"It isn't a riddle, Mia. And deep down, I think you know exactly what I mean." Lucifer braced his hands on

27

the table and stood. "This all goes back to you and Az, your connection, and an oath *you* once swore."

My heart pounded against my ribs. Voice a whisper, I answered. "An oath I once swore?"

"Oh yes," he hissed back, his eyes flashing. "You're not the innocent little thing you think you are, Mia. In your past life, you were wicked, cunning, and sometimes cruel."

Tears filled my eyes. I shook my head and stumbled away from the table. "That's a lie. I don't remember everything, but I do remember the entire year I spent with Az. There was nothing wicked in that. Everything about that was good."

Lucifer gripped the sides of the table and leaned forward. "Oh yes. Until you agreed to a deal."

I swallowed hard, blood roaring in my ears. Not this again. Another demon. Another deal. One my past self agreed to. One I couldn't remember. But Lucifer could.

"What was the deal?" I whispered.

At that, Lucifer sucked in a breath and stepped back. He blinked, as if clearing his head. "I've said too much."

Growling, I stormed toward him and jammed my finger into his chest. "Absolutely not. You can't say all that and then not finish it. What was the deal, Lucifer? Who did I make it with?"

"I'll answer one of those questions," he replied. "You made it with the Creator."

I gaped at him. "*What?*"

"The Creator can make deals. So can fallen angels." He winced and glanced away. "It was the perfect move, one I never saw coming. He made you agree to do a wicked thing, and there was little I could do to stop it."

Shaking my head, I stumbled back. "I think I've heard enough."

His gaze sharpened on me. "I thought you wanted to know the truth."

"I don't think I like where this is going."

"The old you *loved* it." Fear and anger churned in his eyes; ash flowed off his bronze skin. "You are nothing like I expected, Mia, because you are nothing like *her*. And yet, somehow, you share the same soul."

I took another step back, but he grabbed my hand before I could escape. Leaning down close, he whispered the words into my ear.

"The Creator offered you immortality."

Eyes burning, I yanked my hand away. "Fallen angels and demons are already immortal."

"It was more than that," he said in a harsh voice. "You're invincible. Indestructible. Ripping out your heart doesn't work. How do you think you're here, Mia? It wasn't an accident. You made a deal, an oath. That's how you came back."

I swallowed hard, fear snaking through my veins. Whatever he was about to say next, I knew I didn't want to hear it. My gut clenched. My heart pounded hard against my ribs. In my past life, I had done something terrible. I knew it deep within my bones.

"What did he want in return?" I breathed.

Lucifer stared deeply into my eyes.

"Tell me." I fisted my hands.

He pressed his lips together, shaking his head. "I will sorely regret it if I tell you."

"You'll regret if you don't because I'll slam my knee into your balls."

He searched my gaze, not even flinching at my

threat. "You have her fire, but she did not have your heart."

"Maybe *your* heart is the one I should rip out."

Alarm flickered across his face, and he quickly took a step back. Fear? From Lucifer? Because of my threat? Interesting.

"You agreed to help him end the world," he snapped, narrowing his eyes. When I gasped, he smiled. "Yes, that's right, Mia. Weren't expecting that, were you? Good, angelic Mia. Teaming up with her demon boyfriend to end the world as we all know it. That's why I've spent every waking moment of my life trying to stop you two from reuniting. Because you will do it together."

4

I pressed my shaking fingers to my lips, and the scent of pizza swirled into my nose. A shocking reminder of reality in the midst of so much terrifying insanity. It took me back to my early Manhattan days, when Serena and I would wander down to the corner shop and order a slice or two of New York's best.

It was hard to imagine how things had gone so wrong. How had I gone from that to this?

"I never would have agreed to do something like that, even for immortality or whatever you want to call it."

"*You* wouldn't, Mia. But your past self would. And she did."

"But I've never heard from the Creator. I didn't fulfill that deal...did I?"

"You died before you could, rendering your contract moot. So, luckily for you, you're no longer bound to that deal."

A long moment passed where all I could do was stare into Lucifer's face. The trouble was, everything he said

31

made sense. It put the pieces into place. The puzzle fit. It explained so much, even though I hated every word of it.

"So, that's why you tried to kill me," I finally said. "To stop the end of the world."

"Partially. I wasn't trying to kill you permanently. I knew that would never work because of your deal. I was just buying myself some time to figure things out. I could have gone after Az instead, but he's one of my Princes. I could never harm him."

I laughed. Tipped back my head and laughed so loud the sound echoed off the black stone walls. Tears even poured down my cheeks at the hilarity of it all. To be perfectly honest, I felt like I was starting to lose my goddamn mind.

"I've never heard so much bullshit in my life," I finally said when I'd wiped the tears from my cheeks. "You expect me to believe that when you literally just offered me a deal to make me rip out his heart?"

"It won't destroy him permanently," he said in a low voice. "He's a demon."

"And he would never forgive me."

Lucifer flashed me his teeth. "Exactly."

Understanding rushed over me all at once. So, this was Lucifer's angle. He didn't care about Az's heart. Not really. He just wanted to rip the two of us apart. If I did this to him, Az would see it as the ultimate betrayal. No amount of reincarnation would bring us back together.

I folded my arms. "So, what you're telling me is that you want to stop the world from ending, and you're willing to stop the game of souls if I do this thing for you. But the thing is, Lucifer, if you really want to save the world, why go through all this? Why not just forfeit now?"

"If only it were that simple," he said softly.

"From where I'm standing, it is."

"There's a prophecy," he said, his eyes flashing. "That you and Az will end everything, regardless of the game of souls. This is the only way to stop you."

My heart pounded my ribs. "A *prophecy*? What kind of insanity is this?"

"I heard it from the Creator," he murmured back. "He knows an Oracle. She told him all about it. That's why he was so willing to make you the deal. It ensures you worked for him, not me. The only problem is, I don't know all of the details."

"Well then why haven't you gone to the Oracle to hear the damn prophecy yourself?" I snapped.

Lucifer let out a bitter laugh. "You think the Creator would let me anywhere near the Oracle? He'd rather join me here in the flames. And trust me. He hates the heat. Ice runs through his veins."

Well...that was weird. But certainly not the weirdest thing I'd heard today.

"So, that's a no to the Oracle then. I'm just going to have to trust what you've said?"

He arched a brow. "Do you really think I'm lying?"

I pressed my lips together. He was the King of Hell, and I obviously couldn't rule out the possibility that this was just a cruel scheme to get me to agree to his offer. But something about his words rang true. It was like a distant memory, hidden in the depths of my mind. It whispered like darkness through me. Obviously, Lucifer still hadn't told me everything. He was hiding some-thing, and I didn't know what.

But he'd laid most of the truth before me.

The girl I'd once been had signed a wicked oath. And it had turned Lucifer against me.

If only I could go back through time and slap myself. Past Me had made things ridiculously complicated.

"There must be another solution. One that doesn't involve ripping out hearts."

Lucifer shook his head and stepped back. "I'm surprised by you, Mia. I thought if you knew the truth, you'd want to do whatever it took to fix it. Not the past you. *This* you. The one with a mortal heart who would never put herself before the rest of the world."

I bristled at that, scowling. "Don't act so high and mighty, Lucifer. You're the fucking King of Hell. You're playing a game for souls and trying to send the world to Hell yourself. You're only doing this because you don't want to lose. Well, maybe the world *would* be better off if this whole thing ended once and for all. Maybe the Creator should win."

He sucked a slow, steady breath in through his nose and closed his eyes. "You have no idea what you're saying."

I squared my shoulders and stepped toward him. "There must have been a reason I willingly agreed to do this. You say I was wicked and cruel, but I don't see how I would have ever risked the fate of the world if I thought the Creator winning was wrong. Don't act like I don't know how this whole thing works. You win, the world's in Hell. The Creator wins, it's Heaven for everyone. I think I know what the better option is."

He chuckled and shook his head. "Ah, Mia McNally. So naive in your mortal body. So unaware of everything.

It's time for me to show you exactly what you've doomed the world to become."

His hand latched on my arm, and suddenly, the world vanished beneath my feet. Darkness consumed me.

🐚

*W*hen I opened my eyes, my breath frosted before me. My cheeks burned but not from heat. Every bone in my body ached from the biting cold. Lucifer held me in his arms, his heavy black wings beating against the air.

With every beat, another blast of cold slammed into my frozen body. My teeth chattered. I couldn't even feel my fingers anymore.

"Where are we?" I choked around my burning lungs. It was hard to blink, let alone speak. The chill was unlike any I'd ever felt before, not even on the coldest winter day.

"This is Heaven, the realm of the angels," Lucifer replied. "The edge of it anyway. I cannot pass the border."

I swallowed hard and gazed around. Everything was covered in frost and ice. There were patches of trees here and there, but their branches were bare and flickering in the harsh breeze. It looked like death had come to claim this land.

"Why is it so cold?"

"Fire and ice. We are polar opposites, unable to coexist in harmony. If we passed this border and went into the very depths of their lands, it would kill me."

I cast a glance over my shoulder. "I thought demons couldn't die."

"They can. By coming here. And vice versa. The angels, unless they're fallen, cannot survive the heat and flames of Hell. It's our protection against them. They can never invade."

I turned back to gaze out at the ice. It went on for miles and miles, vanishing past the horizon. How far did it go? And what else was out there?

"I don't understand what you want me to see," I said. "It's just ice."

"How does the cold feel, Mia?" he murmured, wings still flapping behind him.

"Not great," I admitted.

"This is what the whole world will become. A frozen tundra, devoid of life. The angels will rule over it all. Everything you know and love will be gone. Ice will consume it all."

"I don't understand," I whispered as I lost all feeling in my toes. I tried to wriggle them around in my boots, but nothing moved. "I've been to Hell. Nothing about it felt like this."

"Where there is heat, there is life." He sighed. "I won't lie to you, Mia. The flames are dangerous, and there are creatures in Hell that humans should never encounter. But if the world freezes over, there will be no coming back from it. Life as you know it will end."

Tears filled my eyes as I tried to comprehend it. A frozen wasteland. Nothing and no one but the immortal beings who started it all.

"But why would they want to do this to us? Why would they want it all to end?"

"To start over," he said. "The Creator believes he

made some...mistakes with humanity. He wants to try again. Eons ago, he threatened to wipe it all away. Right near the start. And so I made him an offer. Play a little game for souls. See who won. Keep the world chugging on for a little while longer."

I snorted. "You're actually trying to tell me that you're some kind of hero or something? Please. Don't bother."

"We should take you back. You'll be too cold soon." And with that, the world went dark once more.

❀

*T*he next time I opened my eyes, I found myself on the library floor. I leapt to my feet and started peppering Lucifer with questions. It seemed he'd expected that. He sat in a chair beneath the chandelier, arms cross, head cocked, waiting.

"So, he wanted to play the soul game, but then he still approached me for a deal?" I asked, pacing before him. "Why?"

"I was ahead at the time. He heard the prophecy, and he was afraid I would use you for the win."

"Okay," I said slowly. "And so he wanted me and Az to...what, exactly?"

"Do something that would end the game. Something that would make me lose. Something that would end the world."

I stopped, frowning. "Well, what *is* that?"

He tsked and shook his head. "I'm not going to tell you that because I don't trust you with that knowledge."

"But Past Me knew what that was," I said. "Right?"

He smiled. "Not quite. I killed you before you gained that knowledge."

Things started to click into place. "I can barely remember that day, other than your face when you stabbed me repeatedly in the chest. Thanks for that, by the way. But I was on my way to...somewhere. I was going to..."

"Meet the Creator where he would give you your final instructions." He nodded, and a ghost of a smile whispered across his face. "I intercepted you."

I pressed my lips together. "I see."

"Any more questions?" he asked, brows arched.

"Many."

"Go on then."

"Why is Az against you? If everything you say is true, surely he would be on your side."

"Ah." He closed his eyes and sighed. "Asmodeus doesn't know. Nor does any of his Legion. Caim, Valac, and the others. They believe I'm the monster the entire world thinks I am. Lucifer, the King of Hell, the torturer of human souls."

"But you do torture people here," I said, pointing out the door in the general direction of Hell. "The others, they said that—"

"Hell is a dangerous place. For those who leave our cities. No human souls are tortured inside the safety of Allyria's walls."

"But the Legion said they'd once done terrible things. It made them want to help humanity, to make up for it all."

"False memories."

"Planted by...you."

He nodded.

"But why?"

"Asmodeus once knew the truth. He planned to storm into Heaven and fight. That would have killed him in the process, and I couldn't let him do that. He's my family, and I would do anything to protect him." He sighed, slumping back in his chair. "So, I made myself out to be their villain. They left and never came back."

I shook my head at him in disbelief. "How can you say all that when you're trying to convince me to rip out his heart? You want me to hurt him, so badly that he will never speak to me again, no matter how many lifetimes pass us by. How can he be your family if you're willing to do that to him?"

"Because it's better than the alternative," he said, his eyes vacant and wide. "If we tell him the truth, he'll rush into the ice to sacrifice himself, in order to save us all. His Legion will go with him. Do you know what that means? A dead Legion. A dead Asmodeus. *Permanently* dead. They would never come back from that, Mia. This is the only option. You started this. And now you must end it."

Tears filled my eyes. "You can't honestly expect me to agree to this."

He arched his brows. "Right now? No. Sleep on it. Move the chess pieces across the board and look at the winning sequence. I think you'll come to the same conclusion I have. The only way to win is for you to rip out Asmodeus's heart."

5

Spoiler alert. I didn't feel any better in the morning. Reality felt like the clouds rolling through the stormy skies overhead. Distant, blurry, and unreachable. Maybe someone had slipped some acid into my food, and I was on a really bad trip.

Pretty scary thought, but the alternative was far more terrifying.

This was all real.

Lucifer showed up not long after dawn with a stack of pancakes. I narrowed my eyes at him warily. He seemed to have an endless supply of carbs. Not that I was complaining.

"You know, I really should tell you where to shove that stack of pancakes," I told him as I took the plate and carried it over to the bed. I leapt on top of the soft mattress and began to chow down, not even caring that he still stood in the middle of the floor watching me with an expression halfway between disgust and curiosity. Like I was a wild animal on display. At least I wasn't the one who ate raw meat.

"Have you thought any more about my offer?" he asked.

"Yeah, I've thought about it," I said around a mouthful of pancakes. "And I want to dropkick your offer out the window where it will splat onto the stone ground. Along with you."

His lips quirked. "I think we've established that doesn't work."

I stopped chewing. "If I say no to your fucking deal, will you let me leave Hell and go back home?"

"What do you think?"

"A big fat no."

"Smart girl," he purred.

I nodded. "That's what I thought. You want to think of yourself as high and mighty. Some big hero instead of the villain you are. But you've abducted me, Lucifer. And you won't let me leave. What kind of hero does that?"

"And that is where you misunderstand me."

I arched a brow. "Oh yeah? Because from where I'm sitting, I understand things pretty damn well."

He took a step toward me, his eyes flashing. "I don't care about being a hero. The means justify the ends. I'll do anything to save the world from turning into a frozen wasteland, even if that means I have to do a few terrible deeds."

"That's a horrible justification."

He smiled. "I don't care."

I leaned back, taking another bite of my pancakes. "You really don't, do you?"

"I'm a demon. We live by a different moral standard than you do. You'd do well to remember that."

"Fine. I'll remember it. And I'm still going to say 'fuck you' while I do."

Sighing, he turned away. "I see. I'll give you a few more days to mull things over. You clearly need more time in isolation to understand what you need to do. The world is very close to ending, Mia. Last I counted, we're only six months away from one of us winning. But I suppose that doesn't matter to you."

His boots echoed off the stone walls as he strode toward the door. Gritting my teeth, I released my tight grip on my fork. It clattered against the plate.

"Wait," I said.

He paused, shooting me a sharp glance over his shoulder. "Yes?"

Truth was, Lucifer wasn't the only one willing to do whatever it took. My past self got me into this mess. I needed to step up to the plate now to fix it. As long as I was stuck in this literal hellhole, everything would be at risk.

Everything.

If I had to lie to get out of here, then so be it. If I had to make a deal I knew I'd break, fine. I wouldn't kill Az, but Lucifer didn't know that. Right now, I needed to do whatever it took to get back to Manhattan, so I could tell Az everything. He would know exactly what to do.

"I'll sign your contract." I threw out the words before I could stop myself.

Lucifer beamed. "What an excellent choice. Just one last thing. There is a time limit on my offer. Once you return to Manhattan, you have seven days. After that, your soul is mine."

6

Manhattan. I sucked in a deep breath and filled my head with the stench of the city. Garbage and taxi fumes had never smelled so good. Horns honked, tourists shouted, and dishes clattered. I was home.

Home.

Fear tumbled through my belly, driving away my relief. Lucifer's words echoed in my ears. If I didn't find a way to fix this, one day New York would become a ghost town, the bustling streets covered in ice.

Not one day, I had to remind myself. If I wasn't careful, it would happen far too soon. Six months tops, if Lucifer was to be believed. I had to find a way to stop that from ever happening.

But right now, I needed to focus on my plan, which meant hightailing it to Az's penthouse and telling him everything. Lucifer was wrong. There was only one way to solve this complicated puzzle. Az needed to know everything.

Once he knew, we could gather the Legion together

and make a plan. No one was ripping out anyone's heart. Unless it was Lucifer's, of course. That I would be okay with.

When I reached his building, I bustled straight past the doorman and rode the elevator up to the top floor. Once the doors whirred open, I crossed the hall to his apartment and knocked. My heart banged against my ribs. It had only been a few weeks since I'd seen him, but it felt like years. Time had passed strangely in Hell, and the hardest part of my captivity had been not seeing Az's face. I'd yearned for it all. That wicked glint in his eyes. The way his hand caressed my thighs...

I flushed, memories filling my mind.

The door swung open. Az stood before me in nothing more than sweatpants hanging low around his hips. His chest gleamed beneath the hallway lights, and his ruffled hair made me think of the nights I'd spent wrapped up in his sheets.

I started to launch myself toward him, but the look in his eyes stopped me short. He looked...confused.

Chills swept down my spine.

"Hi," I said instead, shifting on my feet.

He ruffled his hair and glanced at the elevator. "I'm sorry. Who...why are you here?"

My heart dropped. "Az, I..."

His gaze went sharp. "Az? Who the hell are you?"

My heart pounded in my chest as pain ripped through me like a knife. I swallowed hard. "It's me. Mia."

He flicked his gaze across me, and then sniffed. I knew what he was doing. Finding out what I was and what I was feeling. Lucifer had found a fae to put another scent glamor on me, believing I'd be able to fulfill the terms of the contract if I smelled like a super-natural instead of a human, which had been my scent glamor before this one. That should have been my first warning sign.

"I've never met you before," he said with a frown.

Those words were a knife in my heart.

Suddenly, I understood exactly what was going on. Hell, I should have expected it. Lucifer had erased Az's memories of me. He probably thought I'd break the deal as soon as I stepped foot onto the Manhattan streets. And so he'd made it impossible for me to connect with Az. How was I supposed to tell him the wild, bizarre truth when I was nothing more than a stranger to him?

A stranger.

Hurt pounded in my head like a drum. Tears filled my eyes.

"I don't know what's going on, but I'm going to have to ask you to leave," he said with a frown. "And don't come back. If you do, I'll call the cops."

I winced when he slammed the door on my face. The Az I knew never would have used the threat of cops against me. Face damp with tears, I whirled on my feet and rushed back into the elevator. My mind whirred as I tried to make sense of it. Az didn't remember me. I had to find someone who did. And then I had to find a way to restore his memories. *Pronto.*

The last thing I could do right now was focus on the pain ripping through me. I needed to focus. Find a way to fix this.

I retraced my steps to *Infernal*. When I'd come back through the hellgate, no one had been at the club, but at least one of the Legion would swing by before lunch. I sneaked back inside through the back door I'd left unlocked and waited in their meeting room for someone to arrive. I needed Caim. Or Valac. Or Phenex. They would know where to find that damn memory box Az and I had used. It was probably still somewhere inside his penthouse.

As I waited, the frantic beat of my heart refused to slow. Asmodeus had no idea who I was. Lucifer had erased his memories. A master at games.

Wait a minute. He'd erased Az's memories, which meant he'd suspected I'd go straight to him.

Which meant...he'd probably guessed my next steps after that. He knew I'd go to the Legion.

They'd all gone down into the dungeon that night. Every last one of them had vanished. My stomach twisted at the implication. Lucifer had taken the opportunity to wipe Az's mind of me. If he'd trapped the others along with him, he wouldn't have let them go armed with memories of Mia. If they remembered me, they would have mentioned me to Az. Hell, they would have been beside themselves with worry that night I'd vanished.

They would have gone through the hellgate to rescue me.

Lucifer had wiped their minds, too.

Not a single demon would know who I was.

I felt like I'd been punched in the gut by a heavyweight champ, and my eyes burned with a fresh wave of unshed tears. Fisting my hands, I fought the urge to kick the table. This place had become my home. These people were my family, far more than my own had ever been. And Lucifer had ripped them away from me.

Because it was the only way to ensure I did what he wanted me to do.

Well, I would just have to beat him at his own game.

Footsteps thundered on the hallway outside the Legion's meeting room. Eyes wide, I leapt from the chair and searched the room for a place to hide. I couldn't let them catch me here like this. They didn't know me. To them, I'd be nothing more than an intruder, poking my head in where it didn't belong.

Knowing Phenex, he'd threaten to feed me to the fishes.

But there wasn't much inside this room. Just a metal table, a few folding chairs, and an oversized map of Manhattan taped to the wall.

"I smell a wolf," Caim said from the hall.

Alarm throttled my heart. They didn't even have to see me to know I was in here. So much for hiding under the table. Demons and their damned enhanced senses.

Bracing myself, I laced my hands and pasted on my best hopeful yet confused expression. Az could smell my emotions, but I didn't think the others could. At least, I hoped not. Otherwise, they'd pick up on my clear distress within two seconds of stepping inside this room.

Caim strode through the door, and his gaze zeroed in on me. Curiosity flickered in the depths of his eyes, and thankfully, I didn't spot a hint of anger. Not until Phenex strode in. His face reddened until it matched his flaming hair, and a growl rumbled from his throat.

"What the hell are you doing in here, wolf?" Phenex barked out as he squared his shoulders.

I shifted uneasily on my feet. "I'm sorry. I'm, uh...." Frantically, I searched my mind for something clever. Anything, anything at all. A part of me wanted to tell them the truth, but I didn't think they'd listen to me any more than Az had. I needed some time to convince them they could trust me while I searched for that black box to restore their memories. But most importantly, I needed to get out of here before they tossed me into the dungeons or something worse.

So, I said the first thing that popped into my head. "I'm here about the job."

Hopefully, they hadn't filled my role in my absence. With my disappearance, they would be a dancer down. Not that they would have remembered why.

Caim and Phenex exchanged a weighted glance. A chill swept down my spine. Uh oh. Maybe I'd said the wrong thing.

Slowly, Caim turned back toward me. His expression was nonchalant, but I could see some tension radiating off his muscular frame. "How did you know about the job opening?"

I shrugged. "I was here partying the other night and overheard a few people talking about it. Plus, I noticed one of the cages was empty."

Please, for the love of sanity, let one of the cages be empty.

"What people?" Phenex demanded.

"Um, I don't really remember. It was a couple of guys, but I couldn't tell you who they were. I was drinking and dancing and wasn't paying a load of attention to it. Just remembered hearing them say they really needed to find a new dancer soon." I cocked my head. "Why? Did I hear wrong?"

"I bet it was Bael," Phenex muttered. "He never knows when to keep his mouth shut."

Caim held up a hand, his curious eyes flicking across my face. "What's your name?"

"My name is *Mia*," I said, half-hoping it would jog their memories. Surely I was somewhere inside their minds. I wasn't entirely sure how the memory loss thing worked, but I was pretty sure the spell didn't entirely erase things. Just...hid them, kind of. And Caim, out of all of the demons, had become like a brother to me. Desperation rose up inside me like an iron fist. I wanted to grab his shoulders, shake him, and scream, 'Don't you remember me?!'

But I couldn't do that unless I wanted them to think I was a crazy person.

Caim's face remained blank, and he held out a hand. "Name's Caim. Nice to meet you, Mia. I suppose you know what kind of club this is since you've been here before. And you understand what the job entails?"

Disappointment rattled me, but I nodded and shook his hand. "Dancing in one of the elevated bird cages. Four hours a shift, or something like that."

"It can be a little unnerving," Caim warned. "There are no breaks. Once you're in the cage, that's it for the night. You have to dance until your shift ends. With how crowded the club gets, we can't lower the cages until it clears out a bit. You up to something like that?"

"Caim," Phenex muttered from behind him, clasping a hand on his shoulder. "Let's chat outside." He shot a glare at me. "The wolf stays in here."

Swallowing hard, I watched the two demons drift into the hallway. They left the door open, thankfully, and their words drifted in to meet my ears.

"You can't honestly mean to give her the job," Phenex said in a low, dangerous voice. "She's an intruder."

"Oh come on, Phenex. I know you want to see everyone as an enemy, but look at her. Hardly threatening. And she looks like she needs our help."

I frowned at the whole 'hardly threatening' bit, even if it was the truth.

Phenex grunted. "She sneaked into our meeting room. What if she's some kind of spy for you know who? Looking to find dirt on us? Az said the king's getting suspicious of what we're doing here."

"A werewolf would never work for Lucifer," Caim whispered. "And besides, we can have Valac take a look at her. If she's against us, he'll be able to read it."

Alarm squeezed my heart. Hands fisting, I took a step back from the door and tried to keep my breathing as calm and steady as possible. Shit. *Valac*. I'd forgotten about his weird power. He couldn't read my actual thoughts, but he could do something close enough to give me trouble. The second he looked at me, he'd know there was more to my story than I'd said.

It was fine. Everything was fine. No need to panic. All I needed to do was convince these two that I wanted the damn job, just so I could get out of here alive. It wasn't like I would take it if they offered it to me. Az had seen me already. If he found me here, he might actually combust. The little job story was just a way for me to get away from Phenex before he did something drastic.

I'd never even have to meet Valac until I got my greedy little hands on the memory box.

What would I do as soon as I got out of here? No fucking clue. I was winging it at this point.

The demons stepped back inside the meeting room. Caim gave me a lazy smile, but the scowl remained on Phenex's face.

"How would you feel about an audition, Mia?" Caim asked.

Relief whooshed through me. I smiled back. "An audition? That sounds great."

Then, I will run out of here as fast as my little feet can manage.

"Good." He slung his hands into his jean pockets and rocked back onto his heels. "Come on then. We'll take you to the floor, and you can get yourself ready to dance. We'll just need to wait a few minutes before you start."

My heart thumped.

"Why's that?" I asked in a small voice.

"We're not the ones who can hire you, I'm afraid. Only the owner can."

"The owner," I repeated numbly.

"Asmodeus." Caim's smile widened as he motioned me to follow him into the hallway. "Don't worry. He's on his way."

7

P henex took my elbow and ushered me down the
hallway. A desperate urge to bolt turned my legs
to jelly. I hadn't really thought this through, and
my little charade was going to come crashing down on
me any minute now. The second Asmodeus saw me,
he'd toss me out. Or worse.

"Listen," I said as we approached the door leading
into the main section of the club. "I think maybe I've
made a mistake."

Phenex's hand tightened on my arm. "Is that so?"

I swallowed hard. "Yeah, I can see that you aren't
super into the idea of hiring a new dancer, so maybe it's
just best if I go home now."

Not that I had a home anymore. I'd lost that
Brooklyn apartment, the one Az had found for me.
Before that, I'd stayed with him or Valac. And before
that, Serena. Lucifer had gotten to her, too. I was sure
of it.

No one in this city had a clue who I was.

"You sure have changed your tune," Phenex grumbled as he kicked open the door with his massive black boot. "I'd say I'm surprised, but I'm not. You're clearly hiding something, and Az will find out exactly what that is."

"Phenex, come on." Caim sighed. "Stop berating the poor girl."

But Phenex just ignored him. He dragged me into the expansive, quiet club and deposited me in front of the birdcages that were parked on the marble dance floor. He motioned toward the nearest cage, the one I'd always used. So, they hadn't replaced me then. Interesting.

Surely Az would have wanted to find another dancer by now.

"Go on then." He nodded toward the cage. "Get inside."

An eerie sensation prickled the back of my neck. I didn't like his tone of voice. As much as I loved the Legion, including Phenex, I knew what he was like. He was fighting for the right side and trying to do good in this world, but he was still very demony as far as I was concerned. Especially toward anyone he considered an enemy.

He wouldn't hesitate to destroy me if he thought I meant any of them harm.

I folded my arms. "I said I've changed my mind. I don't want to audition anymore."

"Too bad," he shot back. "Get inside the cage now, Mia."

I flicked my eyes toward Caim. He merely shrugged. "Might be best to just do what he says."

My heartbeat pounded in my ears. Hands slick with sweat, I backed toward the cage and eyed the exit on the opposite side of the room. If I booked it, maybe I could make it out onto the streets before they could stop me. Of course, I knew this area all too well. This block of Hell's Kitchen was eerily empty when the club wasn't open to patrons. No one would be out there to hear my screams before the demons dragged me back inside.

Caim was right. Maybe I'd better do what Phenex said.

Slowly, I took a step back and ducked inside the cage. Phenex slammed the door on me and shoved the key in the lock.

Click.

I swallowed hard at the glint in his eye.

"You look pretty nervous for someone who's supposed to be here for a job," he sneered through the cage doors.

"Yeah," I said, calling upon every ounce of courage I had. I would need it all if I was going to get through this intact. "Because you've just locked me in a fucking cage."

"If you've got nothing to hide..." He stepped back. "Then, I'll let you out. Easy peasy."

I rolled my eyes. Nothing about this was going to be easy peasy. Just as I opened my mouth to shoot back a retort, a strange shiver went down my spine. Shadows whorled in from the doorway on the opposite side of the room, and Az strode in with danger in his eyes.

He glared up at me as he stalked across the floor, but he didn't look surprised. And he definitely didn't look like he'd forgotten about my little visit. Valac trailed in behind him like a whisper on the wind. His bleached white hair fell into his eyes as he gazed up at me. A shudder went through my gut. Layer after layer of my skin felt pulled back, revealing everything.

I really hated when he did that.

"What the hell is she doing here?" Az barked as he joined Phenex and Caim just outside the cage.

I tried to meet his eyes, hoping that if he looked into the depths of me, like Valac was, he'd see past whatever Lucifer had done to him and recognize me for exactly who I was. But he avoided my face.

Caim's brows shot up. "You know her?"

"Hardly." Az frowned. "She showed up outside my penthouse earlier."

A lazy grin spread across Phenex's face. "Well, isn't that interesting."

Caim frowned and shot an uneasy glance my way. "Really? What for?"

"She acted like I should know her," Az said. "Smelled...upset. And confused. And angry. Like now."

He didn't mention anything about desire. I wondered if he'd smelled that, too.

All four demons turned their focus on me. Heat swirled around me, enveloping my skin. I hugged my arms to my chest and tried to hold back the fear. Az and I had a bond unlike anything I'd ever had with anyone else, but that bond meant nothing if he didn't know me.

"Why are you here?" Az demanded, his commanding voice echoing through the empty club. "What is your purpose?"

"I..." Should I tell him the truth? Would he believe me if I did? Or would it only push him away? Lucifer had tasked me with ripping out Az's heart. Coming from someone he didn't know—at least that he could remember—he might think it was some kind of trick. I needed to earn his trust. Otherwise, he might never let me use the memory box on him. "I'm in a bit of a pickle."

His brows arched. "A pickle?"

I nodded, an idea forming in my mind. I'd give him as much of the truth as I could. The truth I'd run from for the past three years of my life. Funny how it might be my saving grace now.

"Yeah, so, um." I shifted on my feet. This was hard for me to say out loud. I'd discussed this whole thing with Az once before, but things were different now. Then, he had known me, if only for a little while. It had felt right. The way he looked at me now made me feel like a bug beneath his boot.

He folded his arms. "You have five minutes to explain yourself. After that, I'll lose my patience with you."

"What happens when you lose your patience?"

"You probably don't want to find out," Caim said with a wince.

"Okay." I sucked in a deep breath. "I'm homeless and jobless and have nowhere to go. My parents won't let me move back home because they think I ran someone over with my car and left them to die alone in the street. I didn't, by the way," I said quickly when I saw Az's eyes darken. "Someone else did it. Someone I wanted to protect, so I never said a word. And every time I try to get a job, they look me up and see the charges. I only got off on a technicality, so they just assume I did it. No one wants someone like me working for them. I'm a liability."

The words stung less than they had before. Once, it had been impossible for me to talk about it, even with

Serena, who knew everything. I'd kept it all bottled up inside, letting it fester in my heart. Until I'd met Az, the Legion, and the dancers at *Infernal*. They'd all accepted me for who I was, no questions asked. When I said I didn't do it, they'd believed me when no one else had.

Az rocked back on his heels, his expression unreadable. "If all that is true, why would you expect me to feel any differently about your past than everyone else?"

This is where I needed to be careful. I only knew he'd accept me because he'd proven it to me before. That and the fact the Legion liked to protect the supernaturals of the city. They looked after their own. They stalked the streets, taking down bad guys. But I obviously couldn't let on that I knew more about his little operation than I should.

I let my hands drop heavily to my sides. "Because I'm desperate."

Az sighed and turned to Valac, who was almost drenched in shadows now. "Well?"

He nodded, his luminous eyes pouring across my face. "She's telling the truth."

"I see." Az turned back to me. "I suppose we should let you audition then."

"Boss," Phenex interjected. "I don't think this is a good idea. Even if she's telling the truth, I don't think she can be trusted."

Az clapped his hand on Phenex's shoulder. "I'll let her audition. And then we'll take it from there."

Ominous. Still, I'd won a hand if not the entire game. And now I had to dance my ass off. I needed to show them what I could do.

Even though I'd pulled the job excuse out of my ass, the truth was...it would make this whole thing a hell of a lot easier if I actually got it. I could get close to them all, get them to trust me. It would be money in my pocket, food in my belly, and a roof over my head. All while I searched for the magic box to restore their memories of me.

And then we could find a way to stop Lucifer. Together.

First things first, I had to pass this audition. The cage rolled up from the floor, shaking on its thick metal chain. Music blasted from the speakers, and the demons stepped back to watch me do my thing.

With a deep breath, I closed my eyes and let the music fill my soul. It drove away my fear and anger, grounding me in the present. I lifted my arms to my sides and danced. My body moved as if by instinct. The notes rang in my head and blocked out everything else.

When it stopped, it was like I reached the surface after a deep dive into the depths of the ocean. I sucked in a breath and flipped open my eyes, trembling from the intensity of it all. The demons all gazed up at me. Az's lips curled into a smile. He began to clap.

They lowered the cage to the floor, though Phenex made a few grumbling noises about it. Timidly, I held my breath and waited for Az's reaction. Would this be like last time? Az had liked my dancing then, but he still hadn't given me the job until the following day. That normally wouldn't be a problem, but I didn't have a day to waste.

Seven days. Lucifer's words rang in my ears. *One week*.

"Very good," Az murmured, his lips still curled into a wicked grin. "You're a natural."

"So, does that mean I got the job?"

He rubbed a hand against his jaw, considering me. "The thing is, Mia. I believe your story, but I still don't trust you. How did you find my penthouse? Why did you act like I should know who you are?"

I flushed. "I've been to this club before. Several times. I thought you might have recognized me...and I found your penthouse because everyone in the supernatural community knows where you live. All I had to do was ask around."

His eyes narrowed. "I wouldn't say everyone."

"Enough people do," I argued.

"And how did you know about the job?" he asked. "We haven't advertised it yet."

"Just like I told the others." I motioned toward Caim and Phenex. "I heard a couple of guys talking about a job the last time I was here. And I noticed the empty cage. It didn't take a rocket scientist to figure it out."

He shook his head. "You may have an answer for everything, Mia, but I still don't trust you. There's something you're not saying. I can see it in your eyes. Valac senses it, too."

Frustration boiled in my gut. If he wouldn't trust me about this, he wouldn't trust me about *anything*. If only I could travel back to Hell and punch Lucifer right in his smug face. He'd made this all horribly impossible.

On purpose.

"That said," Az said after clearing his throat. "I'm willing to give you a chance."

I sucked in a sharp breath and lifted my chin. "Really?"

The way he'd been talking, I really hadn't expected that.

"The job is yours. For now."

The corners of my lips lifted into a smile.

"But when you are not dancing at the club, you will be confined to my penthouse." He strode toward the cage and glared at me through the bars. "Where I can keep an eye on you."

8

My heart pounded in my chest as I met his gaze. "Confined to your penthouse. Like a prisoner? Don't you think that's a bit much?"

A familiar wicked smile flickered across his lips. "If it's a bit too much, then you're welcome to walk out of here."

Honestly, I was tempted. Working at *Infernal* was a pretty fantastic way to get close to the Legion, but it came at a price. I'd be stuck either here or at Az's penthouse. *All the time.* That didn't give me the freedom I needed to sort this thing out.

Of course...maybe I didn't need freedom. The last place I saw the memory box was at Az's place. It was probably still there. As soon as I found it, I could use it on him and the rest of the demons. Maybe this could all be over as soon as tonight.

Wouldn't that be amazing?

He arched a brow. "Well?"

I held my breath and glanced at the others. Phenex

scowled at me, clearly unimpressed by Az's offer. Valac stared in that vacant way he had while Caim full-on grinned. He was having a lot more fun than the rest of us were.

"Sure," I finally said. "If that's what it takes."

"Good." Az nodded and motioned for Phenex to release me from the cage. A part of me couldn't help but wonder what would have happened if I'd turned him down. Would he have let me go like he'd said? Or would it have been dungeon life for me?

Good thing I never had to find out.

After Phenex unlocked the cage, he and the others vanished from the main room of the club, leaving me alone with Asmodeus. He stood just before me with his arms crossed, eyes hooded. He might have given me the job, but he didn't look very happy about it.

"You're a curious thing," he said quietly. "Want to explain to me how you seem so at ease around a group of demons? Most wolves don't like us."

Because I'm a human with the soul of a fallen angel. And I know you.

"I guess I'm not most wolves."

"No," he murmured. "You're not. When were you changed?"

Blood rushed into my ears. The entire problem with pretending to be a werewolf was that I didn't have the experiences to back it up. All I knew was what I'd seen from Serena, which would only get me so far. Watching someone else shift wasn't the same thing as experiencing it yourself, just like most things in life. As much as we want to understand someone else's world, we never truly do until we walk in their shoes.

"I don't actually remember," I said, shrugging. "I was a kid, and it's all a bit of a blur."

That was what Serena always told me.

"Hmm. And no Packs took you in?"

"Nope. That's why I'm here."

"Well, in that case, let's get you settled in to your new home." He glanced down at my empty hands, as if suddenly realizing I'd come here with nothing but the clothes on my back. "Where are your things?"

I didn't have any things. Well, I did, but who knew what had happened to them. I doubted my old landlord would have put them into storage, and everything else had been at Valac's. That had only been a small selection of clothes. I doubted they'd hung onto them.

"I'm afraid all I've got is me."

He shook his head and led me through the hallway toward the front door. When we pushed out onto the streets, a sudden *zing* went through me. I sucked in a breath and glanced up at Az. It had been awhile since I'd felt the sting of our connection, and I'd never been happier to feel it than now. It was still there. A reminder of what we meant to each other.

Az's head jerked to the side, and he frowned.

My heart thumped.

He'd felt it.

Unfortunately, he didn't seem to want to acknowledge it. Yet. But it was a good start. The first step toward getting him to trust me. Maybe. Or he'd just think I was trying to put a spell on him.

We took a car to his building and rode up the familiar elevator. When he ushered me inside his penthouse, I tried to calm my racing heart. It looked just as it had before

Lucifer had dragged me to Hell. Glittering, expensive, starkly elegant. The floor to ceiling windows opened onto a balcony that looked across the New York City skyline.

Tension pounded in my head as Az rounded me with a frown. "Interesting. You look as though you've seen a ghost."

I pressed my lips together. My emotions were giving far too much away, but there was nothing I could do about it.

"I need to get something from my room. Stay here," he commanded. "If you try anything, I'll know."

Az vanished into his bedroom, and I let out a pent-up breath. This whole charade was turning out to be far harder than I'd ever expected. There were so many things that could trip me up, my emotions most of all. But I'd just have to make it work. There was far too much at stake to give up. If I didn't get through to Az and the Legion, I'd lose my soul. And Lucifer would never stop the game that would be the end of humanity.

No pressure, right?

As I padded into the living room, a bundle of white feathers charged in from the balcony. Hendrix spun toward me, landing squarely on the coffee table. The pigeon blinked at me, and I swore I felt him smile. Clearly, I was hallucinating.

He cocked his head and cooed. Grinning from ear to ear, I scurried over to him and ruffled his feathers. "Hendrix. You're still here? Az has been looking after you all this time?"

He blinked at me. If only pigeons could speak.

How was this even possible? Without memories of me, Az wouldn't know that Hendrix was...well, my pigeon, kind of. Why would he adopt a random New

York City bird? I glanced out at the balcony. A bowl of ripped-up bread sat on the wrought-iron table.

Az strode back into the living room with a fluffy robe and a towel in his hands. He took one look at me petting Hendrix and dropped everything to the floor. A dumb-founded look crossed his face; his eyes blinked a million miles a minute. And then he seemed to collect himself, bending over to gather the towel and robe.

I'd never seen him that caught off guard.

"Everything okay?" I asked slowly.

"That pigeon has been the bane of my existence the past few weeks." He chuckled and cocked his head. "He won't go away, but every time I try to get near him, he pecks at my hands. Same with the rest of my Legion. I thought there was something wrong with him...but he's clearly taken by you."

I couldn't help the smile that swallowed my face. Hendrix had been terrorizing Az in my absence. Good boy.

"What can I say?" I smiled. "I'm good with animals."

"Of course you are." His smile turned vicious. "Although, it's interesting. Most animals aren't keen on wolves, especially birds. You're predators."

Unease clenched my heart. Dammit. He was right. Hendrix had been fine with Serena, but that had only been because we'd fed him scraps for weeks. At first, he'd been timid as hell when she'd tried to pet him. The scent of her wolf drove him away.

"Interesting place you have here," I said, changing the subject. "Very fancy. Nice view, too. Your club must do pretty well for you to afford a place like this in Hell's Kitchen."

"*Infernal* isn't my only asset." He trailed over the

kitchen and grabbed two glasses from the bar. "I've been around a long time. Over time, the earnings add up. Would you like a gin and tonic? You look like that kind of girl."

Deja vu flashed through me. He'd said that the day we'd met.

"Yeah, I'll take one." I could use it. This day had frayed my nerves, and I could use a little liquid courage. I'd conquered the first step in my hastily-scrabbled-together plan. I'd made it inside his penthouse. Now, I just had to find that memory box.

He poured two drinks and crossed the floor. When he pressed the glass into my hands, our fingers brushed. That *zing* went through me. It lit up my insides, squeezing my core. My face flushed as I took in his familiar angular face. He looked like he'd been carved from the gods, and the last thing I wanted was this strange tension between us. He stood just in front of me, but it felt like he was miles away.

I'd never been more desperate for someone's touch.

"Cheers," he murmured, clinking his glass against mine.

"What are we toasting?" I asked as I lifted the glass to my lips.

A wicked grin curled his lips. "Your captivity."

9

I frowned and stepped back. "My captivity?"

"I told you I don't trust you, Mia." He smiled. "And that you cannot walk out of this apartment unless I accompany you. This might be a pretty penthouse, but it's more a cage than a home. At least for you. Every move you make, I'll know about it."

"So, you honestly plan to stand watch over me twenty-four seven?" I rolled my eyes. "Please. You have to sleep sometimes. You have things to do, people to see. A business to run."

"I have wards in place." Still smiling, he took a sip of his drink. "If you leave, they'll alert me immediately. Run, and I'll find you. I know your scent, and I can easily track you down. Not that you would get very far."

I bristled and tightened my grip on the glass. "This is ridiculous."

"I told you this was the deal when I offered you the job," he countered, arching a brow. "Surely it shouldn't be a problem unless you have something to hide."

"I think it's pretty damn normal not to want to be

71

someone's prisoner." I turned toward the balcony and wildly waved at the city. "Maybe I'd like to go grab some lunch. Or have a bagel and a coffee while I take a stroll through the park. Or go shopping for some clothes since I don't have any."

I'd been wearing what I had on for over a week. There are no clothing stores in the deserts of Hell. And it wasn't like Lucifer had given me a chance to pack a few extra t-shirts before he'd dragged me through the hellgate.

"I can get you anything you need," he said smoothly, nodding toward my drink. "Aren't you going to drink that? The ice will melt soon. No one enjoys the taste of watered down gin and tonic."

"I've lost my appetite for alcohol," I said flatly. "And frankly, anything else you could offer me."

"Fine with me." He reached for the glass. "I'll drink yours if you don't want it."

I stepped back and turned away, keeping the drink out of his reach. Lifting the glass to my lips, I downed the entire thing in one gulp. And then I shot him a satisfied smile. Take that.

"You only drank that because I said I wanted it," he said.

"You're smarter than you look."

"A fiery little thing, aren't you?" He chuckled. "Would you like another?"

I *would* like another, but somehow, we'd fallen back into our old rhythm. The one we'd had when we'd first met. He antagonized me. I hurled insults at him. It was like we'd gone back in time, and we were dancing our old dance. It brought an electric fire to my veins, but I still ached for the moments when we'd pushed past all this and opened up our hearts.

I missed the way he looked at me.

I sighed. "Sure. I guess so."

He smirked like he'd won, but the truth was, we'd both lost. He just didn't know it yet. As he trailed over to the bar again, I followed. I leaned against the dining table, folded my arms, and tried to find the words to explain why I was here.

"Why don't you trust me?" I finally asked.

He poured a shot of gin into both glasses, his back facing me. "Seems self-explanatory, Mia. You showed up outside my penthouse and acted like you knew me. And then there was your audition. We had a job opening, but we hadn't advertised it yet. Somehow, you knew when no one else did. I'd like to know how."

I pursed my lips. Maybe it was time I tried to tell him. Was it too soon? Should I wait a bit?

I only had seven days, and half of one had already passed me by. *Too soon* wasn't really an option.

"How would you feel if I said we've met before?" I asked, my heart thumping painfully in my chest. "But you don't remember because someone erased your memories."

"I'd say that sounds like a stretch." He lifted the glasses from the bar and turned toward me. A dangerous glint flickered in the depths of his eyes. "Who would have erased my memories?"

I swallowed hard. "Lucifer?"

"Careful," he warned. "Lucifer is my king."

Right. So, he didn't want to tell me about the Legion's quest to save the souls of Manhattan. I wasn't really surprised. As far as he knew, I could be a spy. This could all be another one of Lucifer's traps. A way to get Az to admit what he was really doing. If he didn't trust me enough to let me wander the streets alone, he wouldn't trust me enough to tell me where his true loyalties were.

"Well, maybe it was another demon then," I said, taking the offered drink. This time, I took just a sip. The gin curled across my tongue, the bitters a heady mixture of cinnamon and cloves. "Someone who doesn't like you very much."

"If you want me to believe I should let you go, you're doing a terrible job of it." His eyes flashed. "It sounds like the story one comes up with when the truth is too terrible to admit. Which means you really are hiding something big from me. And I intend to find out exactly what it is."

I let out a growl of irritation as my emotions got the better of me. "You're impossible."

"Not as impossible as you." He erased the distance between us, towering over me. Shadows pulsed from his skin and rippled across my cheek. I fought the urge to shudder. "There's something not right about you, Mia. And the more you try to explain yourself, the more sure of it I am."

Heart pounding, I took another gulp of my drink. I should have known he'd never listen to what I had to say. It sounded absolutely crazy.

"You know what? Fine. I was just messing around anyway." I turned away and trailed over to the open sliding glass doors that led out onto the balcony. The New York city air filled my lungs, cooler now that fall was on its way. It ruffled my hair, tossing it around my face. Out of the corner of my eye, I caught sight of the brown. I really missed the red, but I hadn't had a chance to undo the fae's glamor.

Az stepped up beside me, tension pouring off his body like the waves against the shore. "You weren't messing around. I can tell by the look on your face. How many lies are you going to tell me tonight?"

"What if I told you something terrible is going to happen if you don't listen to me?"

"I'd say you're desperate." He glanced down at me. "I don't blame you. It sounds like you've had a hard life, and this situation isn't ideal. But at least you have a roof over your head now. You won't go hungry. I'll buy you some new clothes. As far as prison sentences go, you have it pretty damn good."

I rolled my eyes. "Of course you would think that you're doing me a favor. What's next? Getting me to sign a demon contract?"

"Actually, that's not a terrible idea," he mused. "Would you sign one swearing you will never harm me or mine?"

"In exchange for my soul?" I asked him.

He chuckled. "Of course, Mia. That's what demon contracts are."

My heart pounded in my ears. Was this the answer? The way to get him to trust me? Not long ago, I'd been absolutely, one-hundred percent, totally done with demon deals. I'd never wanted to look at another contract in my life. Until Lucifer had forced me to sign one.

And now another was being presented to me.

Fisting my hands, I turned to him. "If I signed it, would you trust me?"

"Not entirely," he murmured. "But it would be a start."

I let out a heavy sigh. "Sure, why not? At this point, what's the worst that could happen?"

"You could lose your soul."

Yeah, but my soul was already on the line, and this wouldn't make it any worse. What was one more deal at this point? At least there was no threat of failing this one. I'd never do a damn thing to harm any of them.

"Okay, I'll sign it."

Az glanced down at me, his eyes slightly widening. "You're serious, aren't you? Interesting. I didn't expect you to agree to it."

"See?" I pointed out. "I'm not the enemy you think I am."

"Maybe not, but you are hiding something."

"Everyone is hiding something, Az." I sighed.

"See, that." He pointed at me. "This is a perfect example of why you're giving me red flags. You barely know me. I've never told you to call me Az."

I shrugged. "Maybe it's actually evidence that we've met before."

"Hmm." He didn't seem convinced, but at least the tension in his shoulders had relaxed a bit. Standing tall beside me, he took the last sip of his gin and tonic and gazed out at the city. Night had begun to fall, signalling the end of my first day back in the mortal world. Truth be told, it had gone a lot better than I'd expected after finding out Az's memories were gone. I was back inside the fold, even if none of them trusted me. Yet.

But I needed to move fast if I wanted to beat Lucifer's deadline. Next step? Find the memory box.

"So," I said, taking a deep breath and hoping for the

best. "You're clearly well off, and it looks like you're a fan of nice things. Have any art? Paintings...or...objects?"

Az stiffened and lowered his drink to the dining table. "Objects?"

"You know, like...odd sculptures. Modern art or whatever. Something you wouldn't think of as art but clearly is."

"I'm not following," he said blankly.

"Well, a lot of modern art is weird, isn't it? Could be something as simple as a metal flower. Or a plain black box or maybe a..." I searched my brain for anything I'd seen in a modern art museum, but I came up blank. "A dog's water bowl."

A water bowl?!

"A box," Az said, zeroing in on the least strange thing I'd said.

His voice sounded strange, which put my teeth on edge. I'd hoped that my rambling explanation hadn't been specific enough, but I'd clearly put him on high alert. Not great for getting him to trust me, but...maybe, just maybe, this was a good sign. Hopefully it meant he'd found the box.

"Well, anything really. But yeah, a box could work."

Preferably a little black one that could restore memories.

"I think that's enough for tonight." Az grabbed my glass, wound his hands around my arm, and angled me toward the hallway. "It's time for you to go to bed."

"I..." I dug my heels into the floor, but my socks slipped along the smooth surface. "But—"

"Goodnight, Mia," he growled into my ear, sending a wave of goosebumps down the length of both of my arms. When we reached my old bedroom, he shoved me inside and slammed the door on my face.

I propped my hands on my hips and glared when the lock clicked. He'd actually gone and trapped me inside. Wonderful. So much for getting my hands on that box tonight.

In the morning, there was a stack of pancakes waiting for me on the marble counter. Az strode into the kitchen from his open bedroom door, a towel slung low around his hips. Rivulets of water trailed down his bare, muscular chest. I stopped in my tracks.

My entire body went hot. Like hellishly hot. My eyes skipped across his body, drinking him in. My god, he was *beyond* attractive. It was like he was on an entirely different level than the rest of the world. Everything about him. Every single inch...

The flames rushed into my cheeks. Now was probably not the right time to be thinking about his inches.

He had a lot of them.

He smirked at me. "Something the matter?"

"You seem to have forgotten your clothes," I said around a mouthful of marbles. "Not that you need them."

My captivity wouldn't be so bad if he wandered around like that.

A deep chuckle drifted into my ears, like the sound of music. I could curl up in that sound and bask it in for years. Too bad he hated my guts and thought I'd been sent here to spy on him for Lucifer.

"There's something you should know about me," he said with a grin that dimpled his cheeks. "I can scent emotions."

"Oh." I pasted on a shocked face. "Like, all emotions?"

"Oh yes," he practically purred, stalking toward me. "Guilt. Anger. Frustration and fear. But I can also scent—"

"Desire," I finished for him, smugly smiling at the surprise in his eyes. "I know what you're trying to do. Unnerve me. But it's not going to work this time."

He let out a heavy sigh, and that wicked smile vanished. "You're still pretending we've met before, I see."

"It's not pretending when it's the truth."

"How did you know I can scent desire?"

"Because you've told me before." I smiled when Hendrix flew in from the window and landed on the counter beside the pancakes. He blinked at me expectantly. Greedy pigeon.

Still smiling, I grabbed the plate and padded over to the dining table in my socks. Az watched me with hooded eyes. Water dripped down onto the floor around his feet. I tried not to gape at him and instead settled into the chair and dug into my breakfast.

"Stop lying to me," he said in a tone that suggested he was quickly losing his patience with me. So, nothing new.

I took a bite of the fluffy pancakes and fought back a

moan. Delicious. Mouth-watering really. Just like they'd been the last time I'd stayed here. As I dug in, Az stormed away and returned to his bedroom. By the time I'd finished my breakfast, he'd returned wearing a crisp suit and freshly-styled hair.

I wasn't hungry anymore, but Asmodeus looked delicious.

"You're leaving?"

"You need some clothes, and I need to draft a contract." He smiled when my shoulders dropped. "That's right. Did you think I'd forget about that? You're going to sign a demon deal today, Mia. One that will ensure you never harm anyone under my protection."

I opened my mouth to argue, but he was gone before I could. Dammit. Suddenly, the pancakes didn't feel so satisfying in my gut. They were like lumps of rocks, just sitting there, ready to drag me under.

Even though I'd talked a big game the night before, I didn't want to sign another deal, regardless of the terms. I was sick and tired of them.

No matter. By the time Az returned from his errands, I'd hopefully have a memory box in my hands. Maybe I could wait by the door and throw it at him before he knew what was coming. I'd have to be fast. The only way to pull it off was to catch him off guard.

But first, I had to find the damn thing.

Pushing back my empty plate, I stood and gazed around the penthouse. Hendrix charged in, pecking up the chunks I'd left behind for him.

If I were a demon, where would I put a strange, little black box I'd found on my floor? There was a chance he'd thrown it out, not understanding what it was, but I had a sneaking suspicion he hadn't. Az was a lot of things, one of which was intuitive as hell. He'd take one look at that black box and know it was important.

If we were lucky. And one thing I'd learned during the past few months was that luck and I weren't friends.

My socked feet whispered across the floor. When I reached his bedroom, I tried the knob. The door was locked.

"Dammit," I muttered, whirling on my feet. I needed something to get this door open. My eyes caught on my heavy black boots sitting by the apartment's entrance. Hmm.

No, I couldn't. That would really piss him off. But, at the end of the day, would it really matter? By the time he discovered what I'd done, he'd have his memories—*all* of them—and he wouldn't hold it against me. Hell, he'd be *glad* I did it.

Before I could talk myself out of it, I pulled on my shoes, hauled back my foot, and slammed it into the door. The wood cracked, splintering. With a creak, the door slowly swung open.

The ebony room enveloped me like a warm, familiar hug. Az's curtains were shut against the city lights, and shadows rippled across the silk sheets, reminding me of him. The scent of fire filled my head, drowning out everything else. With an aching heart, I glanced around.

All I wanted was to climb into that bed and wait for his return. He'd see me draped in his sheets, and everything would suddenly come back to him. His body would cover mine, and his lips would hungrily kiss my skin until our bodies were so wrapped up together that I wouldn't know where I ended and he began.

I closed my eyes and shook my head at myself.

Clearly, I needed to get a grip. Now was definitely not the time to daydream about demon dick.

Az barely even knew my name.

My desire deflated like a popped balloon. I padded across the floor and pulled open his dresser drawers. If I were a little black box, maybe I'd be in here. I rustled through his soft tees and boxer shorts, trying my best not to get distracted. I knew where these shorts had been...

Focus.

There was nothing in these drawers but clothes. Frowning, I dropped to my knees to peer under the bed. I knew he hid things in this room. He'd kept the door locked every day that I'd lived with him. Even when I'd slept in the bedroom, he'd never let me poke around.

My eyes caught on something black and gleaming. A larger black box...more like a trunk. With a hitch in my breath, I slid beneath the bed, grabbed each edge, and yanked it across the floor.

It weighed about a hundred pounds.

No, *way* more than that. I could hardly move it. Just enough to get a better look.

Heart hammering, I stared at the lock. What the hell could he be hiding in there? Would he have really hidden a little black box inside when he didn't know what it could do? Seemed unlikely. It didn't warrant that kind of protection...

But my curiosity was rattling ahead at top speed. I wanted to know what Az was hiding.

"Mia." The voice jerked me out of my reverie and launched my heart into my throat. Sucking in a deep breath, I jumped to my feet, clutching the first thing I could find. A pair of boxer shorts. *Great weapon, Mia.*

Rafael—or Noah as I used to know him—hulked in the doorframe. He glared at me with gleaming eyes, his hands curled into massive fists. Anger rippled through me. This guy had been the reason so many terrible things had happened. He'd murdered innocents. He'd abducted my best friend. And now he was here.

"What the hell are you doing here?" I hissed at him.

"Lucifer sent me back here to watch you," he said in a growl. "It's a good thing, too, because it looks like you're up to your old tricks. What are you doing in Asmodeus's bedroom? Why haven't you killed him yet?"

My heart thumped. "Well, first, I'm in here because..." Obviously, I couldn't tell him about the memory box. "I'm looking for his sword. And second, I haven't killed him yet because Lucifer erased Az's memories of me. And so he doesn't trust me. I'm only mortal, Rafael. If I can't get close to him, I'll never be able to rip out his heart."

"Hmm." He nodded and glanced around. "You find it?"

I kept my gaze firmly forward and avoided looking down at the trunk. The last thing I wanted was for my fallen angel enemy to get his hands on that damn sword. I wasn't sure it was inside the trunk, but I wasn't about to risk it. Abaddon could definitely be in there. Something important was.

"Not yet." I motioned at the dresser. "Nothing in any of these drawers, which makes me think he might not hide it in here."

"Maybe you need a different weapon. I could find you one." He frowned when I didn't automatically agree. "What's the problem? Don't actually want to kill him?"

"I mean, no. Of course I don't. Ripping out someone's heart is the last thing I want to do, but it's not like Lucifer gave me another choice, now did he?"

Narrowing his eyes, he stalked toward me. "I don't think you're taking this very seriously."

"Oh, trust me. I am." I held up my hands to my sides. "But what am I supposed to do if I don't have a little help? Az doesn't trust me. He's trapped me here inside this penthouse. When I make my move, I have to be sure it will work. Because if I fail, I'll never get another chance."

I ground my teeth together and willed him to believe me. A lot of what I'd said was true. If I really *was* trying to kill Asmodeus, Lucifer had put me in a bit of a pickle. Without a fallen angel's powers, I was at a serious disadvantage.

He sneered. "You know what I should do, Mia? I should wring your neck right here and now. Take you out of the equation. We'd all be better off if I did."

"Lucifer wouldn't like that very much," I said quickly, wetting my lips. "He's sent me here for a reason. A big one."

"I know all about his damn reasons," Rafael snapped back. "But what have you done to fulfill your duty? You only have a week, Mia. And you've already wasted one day."

"It wasn't wasted," I countered. "I went to *Infernal* and got my job back, even though none of them know who I am. That gives me an in. Plus, look at where I am. Az's penthouse. I live here now."

"Good." Rafael's smile was pure evil. "Then, you should take him out in his sleep. That doesn't require any supernatural strength."

Yeah, okay. That did make sense. *Stop talking logic!*

"Az keeps his bedroom door locked. There'd be no way for me to get in without waking him up."

Rafael twisted and looked pointedly at the broken door. "Doesn't look locked to me."

"That's obviously because I kicked it in." I loosed a

frustrated breath. "If I did that in the middle of the night, it'd wake him up. If I'm going to pull this off, I have to sneak up on him when there's no way he can hear or see me before I've done the deed. The only way I can do that is if he trusts me."

"You sure do have a lot of excuses, Mia McNally."

"Luckily, I don't care what you think. My deal is with Lucifer, not with you. A serial killer who targeted my best and oldest friend. As far as I'm concerned, you can rot in Hell. Not the nice city part. The part with the hell-beasts that will rip you apart."

"Leave Serena out of this," he growled.

I smiled. "No, I don't think I will."

Rafael tipped back his head and laughed. "You think you're so clever, don't you? But Lucifer has you trapped. Do as he says, and you'll lose the demon you love. Go against his wishes and lose your soul. Either way, it's over for you, Mia. Meanwhile, I will rule by the hell king's side."

My eyes rolled into the back of my head. "I think I've heard enough. You can go now. Tell Lucifer I'm working on it. I just need another day."

Or two.

A smile whispered across his lips. "The sooner you face the truth, the easier this will be on you. I know what you're really doing here, Mia. You're hoping to get through to Az and warn him about your deal. But it won't work. You'll still lose your soul. The world will still end. And Asmodeus along with it. You'll be far better off ripping out his heart. We all will."

"Asmodeus is a demon," I said with a frown. "If the world ends, he'd survive just fine."

"Not if the Creator wins," he countered. "Haven't you heard? Demons can't survive the ice."

I had heard actually, but I hadn't put two and two together. Lucifer's words were starting to make a lot more sense, dammit. All this time, Az had known he couldn't survive the afterlife if the Creator won, but he'd been sneakily helping him regardless. Going against Lucifer. Protecting potential sacrifices. Taking out supernaturals like Rafael when they posed a threat.

Effectively sacrificing himself for the greater good.

I needed to sit down.

"That's right," Rafael said. "Your demon boyfriend will die no matter what you do. Rip out his heart and he has a chance of coming back. Don't, and...well then you know what happens next."

"You know what?" I said, my hands fisting. "I think I hate every single one of you. You, the Creator, Lucifer. You're all bastards."

"Technically, the truth." He held out his hand to reveal a ring inside his palm. "Take this."

I glared at it. "No, thanks."

He sighed. "You might need it if Asmodeus clocks on to what you're up to."

Frowning, I plucked the ring from his hand and held it up before my eyes. It looked a lot like Az's ring, the one I kept hidden in my pocket. An emblem had been carved into the gold. Twin wings flared wide. "Let me guess. It's got magic."

"Whisper my name while touching the emblem with your fingertip," he said in a grave voice. "It will call me to you. But only use it if you get into trouble."

Brows furrowed, I glanced up at him. "Um, okay. Question though. Why exactly are you giving this to me?

Two seconds ago, you were acting like you wanted to throw me out the window."

"Because I want you to succeed." He shrugged. "You're right. You have no powers of your own, and you don't have a weapon. You're far more likely to die than rip out Az's heart. Lucifer sent me here to watch over you. Unfortunately, that means I need to keep you safe."

I scrunched my brows. "This is weird. I don't like it. You're the asshole who pretended to love my best friend, and then you abducted her. Not to mention all those supernaturals you brutally mur—"

"You've made your point," he cut in sharply. "And I don't much like this situation either. The last thing I want to do is team up with a helpless human who'd rather stab me in the back than admit I'm on the right side of this war."

"I mean, you're obviously not on the right side. Because there is no right side. All of you suck some serious ass."

"You going to take the ring or not?" he grunted.

I glared at him. No, I did not want to take the ring. It felt like giving in. The annoying thing was, I might actually end up needing it. Az didn't trust me. I still hadn't found the damn memory box, and I'd knocked down his bedroom door. Things were going to be tense when he got back.

And I was trapped here.

If Az decided I was the enemy before I was able to restore his memories, I needed an escape hatch.

Just...why did it have to be Rafael? *Ugh!*

"Fine." I snatched the ring and pocketed it. "But don't think I'm happy about this. Or that I'll use it. The

damn ring is just a 'no other option' kind of thing.
Got it?"

"Whatever."

"Don't act so annoyed that I don't want to trust you.
This is just a natural reaction to your fallen angel scum-
miness. If you were a good guy who didn't kill people,
I'd probably like you. Maybe."

"There's one more thing you need to know before I
go," he said, changing the subject. "The deal you made
with Lucifer. It is binding."

"Yeah, I know." I shrugged. "Of course it is. It's a
deal with the actual devil. If it wasn't binding, it would
be completely pointless."

"It's more than that. It means you can't sign any
other deals, even to convince Asmodeus that you aren't
against him, which I know he'll try to get you to do. If
you agree to a conflicting deal, the magic won't let you
sign your own name."

All the blood drained out of my face. "What?"

"You heard me."

Rafael jerked up his head, and his gaze went sharp.
Paling, he pressed his lips together and took a step back.
"He's coming."

My heart lurched into my throat. Hands slick with
sweat, I knelt down and shoved the trunk back under
the bed. "He'll smell you. He'll know you were here.
Dammit, Rafael, why did you have to come into his
fucking penthouse?"

"He'll also see that you smashed down his door. I
think that's the bigger problem here."

I jumped to my feet, my eyes wild. "I'll blame it on
you. That makes the most sense."

A wicked smile spread across his lips. Uh oh. I didn't

like how he was looking at me. "I have an idea. One that means he'll finally let down his guard around you."

I shook my head and took a step back. "I don't think I want to hear your idea. It is probably pretty crazy, considering you're a murderous psychopath."

"Don't worry. It'll only hurt a little." Rafael suddenly vanished into smoke and appeared right in front of me a second later. I opened my mouth to scream, but his fist slammed into my skull before I let out more than a whimper.

❀

I stood on top of Manhattan's tallest building, my wings spread out behind me. The wind whipped across my silver feathers, but it did little to soothe the fear raging in my heart. Lucifer knew about me and Asmodeus, and he was coming for me.

It had been a long time since I'd visited Hell. A decade now, maybe. I thought Lucifer saw me as a friend. But none of that mattered anymore. Now that he knew the truth of what Asmodeus and I could do together.

I would have to fight him. It was the only way. He might be the King of Hell, but I'd been training all my life.

Thunder sounded from behind me, and the heady scent of fire swirled into my head. Sucking in a deep breath, I slowly turned toward him. Lucifer stood before me, body tense, wings flared wide. A gilded dagger glittered in his fisted hand. He smiled.

Terror charged through my soul, but I kept my face blank as I faced off against one of my oldest friends. The one I would have to betray. This was what I'd been working toward all my life. "I knew you would come."

"And you know why." He took a step toward me. "I can't allow you to live, Mia."

"I wish there was another way, but there's not."

"Have you told Asmodeus the truth?"

I squared my shoulders. "No."

"Then surely you can see that what you're doing is wrong." He lifted the dagger and flipped it in his hand as if he'd done it a hundred times before. "You will be the destruction of the world, Mia, and you don't seem to care. Hell, it almost seems like you want it to happen."

"Maybe I do." I smiled.

He blinked, and his hand dropped to his side. I'd surprised him. It wasn't often that anyone surprised the King of Hell. But he wasn't the only one with secrets up his sleeve, plotting away while his enemies fell into the elaborate traps he'd set for them.

"That's a lie," he growled. "You left Heaven. You joined me in Hell and saw everything the world would become from the damn game of souls. You were on my side."

I lifted a brow. "Or was I?"

He shook his head, anger churning in the depths of his eyes. "You wouldn't have. You couldn't. Angels don't lie, not even fallen ones."

"They don't like to lie," I corrected. "But there's nothing stopping them from twisting the truth if it suits a purpose."

Fury was a storm across his face. His entire body trembling, he shouted, "I can't believe I ever trusted you!"

I shrugged. "Neither can I. You've made things far easier for me than I ever expected."

I'd found the truth, only by getting close to him. The Creator had planned to tell me tonight, but I'd already discovered it myself. If I ripped out Lucifer's heart, then I would end the game of souls. But it was not straightforward, ripping out a demon king's heart. It required the power of heaven and hell combined.

An angel and a demon, two halves of the same coin.

Luckily for me, Asmodeus had given me his ring.

Lucifer lifted the dagger before him. "You've made a very terrible decision, Mia. What do you think will happen if you win? Not that you have a chance in Hell of beating me."

I smiled. "I will be greatly rewarded back home."

His eyes searched my face. "Home? You said you never wanted to return to that place."

My smile widened. "Haven't you figured it out yet, Lucifer? Everything I've told you is a lie."

His ground his teeth together. "And Asmodeus?"

I faltered, only for a split second, but it was enough for Lucifer. He nodded, laughing, shaking his head. "That's why you haven't told him about any of this. If he knew the truth, he would hate you."

My mouth dry, I set my lips. "It doesn't matter."

His glittering smile flickered with rage. "I'm going to enjoy this."

"Not as much as I will." Reaching behind me, I drew the sharp sword from the scabbard on my back. The weapon hummed with energy, thirst and rage pouring down the length of it. I'd borrowed Abaddon from Az's stash. If any sword could slice through the King of Hell, it was this one.

"You're in way over your head, Mia. Even with that monstrous sword."

My heart thumped as I bent my knees into a warrior's stance. Lucifer charged, an eerie grin lighting up his face. I screamed as he ducked past my blow and slammed his knife into my chest. It was over before it even began.

1 2

I leapt out of bed, still screaming. Sweat soaked my face, and my heart thundered so hard against my chest that I swore my ribs would shatter. Sucking in deep breath, I tried to will the panic away, but the images from my dreams flickered on frantic repeat.

Everything I thought I knew had been a lie. Lucifer had been right.

We'd only gotten half the truth from the fucking memory box. The reality of my past life was nothing but a lie. A lie I'd told Asmodeus.

I really was the enemy. I'd been trying to end the world.

Az flew into my bedroom, his eyes wild. Abaddon glimmered in his trembling hands. He took one look at my pale, sweat-soaked face, and a heavy sigh rocked his body. He dropped his sword to the ground and gathered me into his arms. I could hear his heartbeat against my ear.

Well. This was certainly unexpected. In the best way possible.

It almost made me forget about the fact that Past Me had clearly been trying to end humanity.

Almost.

"I thought he'd gotten to you again, and this time, I was too late," he murmured against the top of my head. "But it must have been nothing more than a nightmare."

He? Gotten to me? Did he mean Lucifer?

But...

"I can't believe Rafael was bold enough to come into my damn home to attack you," he said in a voice that rumbled in his throat.

Oh. Rafael. In the wake of my fever dream, I'd forgotten all about that little encounter. And the fact he'd literally knocked me out. If it hadn't been an absolutely genius idea, I'd be tempted to track him down and return the favor.

"Did you catch him?" I asked, pulling back to look into his face. "The last thing I remember is his fist slamming into my head."

Speaking of...I reached a hand up to my forehead but didn't feel a thing. No bruise. No pain. No nothing. Had Az healed me again?

Something about that thrilled me all the way down to my toes. If he'd healed me, maybe he didn't hate me that much after all.

"He was gone by the time I opened the door." His eyes flickered with rage. "I started to go after him but then I saw you on the floor. Why were you in my bedroom?"

"He went in there looking for something. I was in my room when he got here, and I heard him kick down your door. When I went to investigate, he cornered me." It didn't take much to put the terror in my voice, making it wobble a bit. I was still unnerved about the whole thing, and the news Rafael had delivered me. And that dream...

His brows furrowed. "Looking for what?"

"I don't know. He didn't really say much to me."

Az released his grip on me and strode over the window. Hands slung into his pockets, he sighed. "Do you know who that was?"

"A fallen angel," I said. "Last I heard, there are four of them in the city. And some of them are killing supernaturals. Probably him, based on what he tried to do to me."

Az glanced over his shoulder at me. "Where did you hear that?"

"Same place I heard where you live." I joined him by the window. "The supernatural gossip mill."

He let out a sigh of relief. "I thought you were going to start up about the memory loss again."

Az had softened to me after Rafael's attack, and I didn't want to push it. "People talk. Things get out eventually, especially things like this. There have been a lot of deaths lately..."

He nodded. "We traced them back to Rafael, but we haven't been able to stop him. He vanishes whenever we get close. Frustrating, really. I've never seen anything like it. But one day, he'll make a wrong move. Today was almost that day. He's too bold, that Rafael. He likes to target supernaturals who are close to me, but coming into my penthouse was a risk I didn't think he was willing to take. If I'd gotten home even two minutes earlier, he'd be dead."

Excitement tripped through my veins. Asmodeus was confiding in me and telling me things he hid from most. Amazing what a little unconsciousness can do to get an angry demon to trust you. Maybe I should have done it sooner.

"Do you know what I think he was looking for?" I said.

"You, I'm guessing," he replied quietly. "Based on his past actions, we've determined he has a thing for wolves."

"Well, maybe. But remember, he went into your room for a reason. I don't think he expected to find me there." I plowed forward without taking a breath. "He said something about a black box. Asked me if I'd seen it before he knocked me out."

This was a *huge* gamble. One I was willing to take. Time was running out, and Rafael was keeping a close eye on me. I needed to find that damn box.

"Interesting." Az shifted on his feet. "And what did you tell him?"

"The truth. I don't know where it is."

"Good." He patted my head...actually *patted my head*. "Let's keep it that way."

I frowned as he pushed away from the window and strode toward the door. "Where are you going?"

"I've brought some clothes back for you," he said in an easy tone of voice that masked his true emotions. There was more going on beneath the surface of his indifference. If only I had the power to scent them. "That and the contract."

Oh yeah. The contract.

I blinked at him. "You still want me to sign that?"

"Of course I do," he said with a frown. "What would have changed?"

"Well, for one, I just got attacked by a fallen angel. Now doesn't seem like a great time to be signing away my soul."

I couldn't sign that contract. If I sat down to do it, the magic would physically stop me from scrawling my name. Which meant I desperately needed Az to let me out of this. The problem was, he was as stubborn as me. And I never would have walked away without a signature if I were him.

Argh!

"Why so hesitant all of a sudden?" He frowned. "This morning, you seemed eager to sign it."

"Well, you read me wrong. I told you once, and I'll tell you again. I'm done signing deals with demons."

Az arched a brow, and his shoulders tensed. "Interesting. Which demons have you signed a deal with before?"

Shit. Heart racing, I took a step back at the fury in his eyes. So much for his softening toward me. Now, he looked like wanted to rip me apart. I may have misspoke. Whoops. It had always been just a matter of time before I'd shoved my boot in my mouth. Lies were tricky things. Tell too many, and they're impossible to keep track of.

He barked out a laugh, but nothing in his expression said he was amused. Furious was more like it. Furrowed brows, tense jawline, shadows whipping up a storm. They moved so fast across his skin that they almost swallowed him whole.

"If I tell you, you won't believe me." I paused, and then said it anyway. "You. You're the demon."

"Nice try," he growled.

"It's the truth."

It *was* the truth, just not all of it.

Growling, he ran a hand through his hair. Power rippled off his body, slamming right into my chest. The force of it caught me off guard and knocked me off my feet. Before I realized what had happened, I was blinking dumbly with my ass on the floor.

Az hurried over to me with panic in his eyes. "Mia? Are you alright?"

"What the hell just happened?" I whispered.

He pressed a hand to my face, his fingers soft against the curve of my jaw. "It's been a long time since I lost control of my power like that. I am so sorry, Mia. Are you alright?"

I blinked up at him, dazed and confused. "You did that?"

"Not intentionally." He gently wrapped his hands around my arms and lifted me to my feet. "The last thing I would ever do is hurt you, Mia."

I stared into his eyes. The fire in them flamed hot, burning away the ice. For a moment, I got lost in them, taken back to a time when everything had been so simple. Me. A demon. Pretending to be in a relationship. Pretending to care. Turned out, neither of us had been pretending. And now he didn't remember a second of it.

Pain ripped through my heart.

He palmed my cheek and sighed. "I've caused you pain. That's the last thing I want to do."

"Really?" I whispered to him. "Because last I checked, you think I'm the enemy. I know what demons do to their enemies."

"You're clearly hiding something, Mia," he said in a

low voice. "But no, I don't think you're my enemy. If you were working for Lucifer, Rafael never would have tried to kill you."

I loosed a breath of relief. The crazy plan had actually worked. "So, you're going to give me my freedom."

"No, I don't think so." Az pulled back, but he did it in such slow motion that it seemed like he had to practically drag himself away. Another *zing* went through my gut. His eyes slightly widened, but he didn't speak a word about it.

"Are you honestly serious?" I propped my hands on my hips and glared at him. "Your weird demon magic knocks me to the floor, after Rafael takes a shot at me, and you're still trapping me inside this fucking penthouse?"

"It's only for a little while, Mia," he said, his eyes shuttering over his emotions. "If Rafael is after you, he'll try again. I'm not letting you out of my sight."

"And you still don't trust me," I added.

A slight smile flickered across his lips. "Tell me what you're hiding, and I'll trust you."

My gut twisted. "I've tried telling you, but you won't believe me. We've met before. Your memories have been—"

"And that's why I don't trust you. You're clinging on to this crazy story instead of telling me the truth." He moved away from me then, halting by my open bedroom door. "Come on then."

I rolled my eyes. "Where are we going?"

"You're going to sign my contract."

A shiver went through me. "No."

"Very well." His smile was razor sharp. "Then, you will sit inside this living room while I stand watch until it's time for us to go to the club for your first shift. I meant what I said, Mia. I'm not letting you out of my sight."

I folded my arms and lifted my chin. "What about when I need to use the bathroom?"

"You may go in there alone, but I'll stand outside the door." He flashed me a smile. "There are no windows in my bathroom so good luck escaping it."

"Where will I sleep?"

"In my bedroom."

"I..." My mouth dropped open, and another blast of deja vu slammed into my chest, causing me to stumble back. Again, he'd done this before. The last time I'd stayed here, Rafael had been after me. Worried the fallen angel would get to me in the middle of the night, Az had insisted that I sleep in his bed.

It was happening all over again, only this time we were far more at odds than we'd ever been.

His eyes softened. "Don't worry. I'm not going to try anything. You'll take the bed while I take the floor."

My stomach dropped. "Oh."

Maybe it wasn't like last time, after all.

"Come on." He motioned for me to join him. "I know you've been wearing those clothes for awhile. Don't you want to shower and change into something clean and fresh and new?"

"Maybe I won't. You know, to stage a protest against this insane behavior."

"If that's what you'd like." He gave me a bemused smile and waited in the hallway for me to move. The annoying thing was, he had me, and he knew it. I'd taken a bath back in Hell, but it had been a very long week travelling through the deserts since then. I felt a bit sticky, and my socks needed a wash.

"Do you really have to stand outside the bathroom door?" I finally said with a sigh.

His cheeks dimpled. "Absolutely."

13

That night, it was time to earn my keep. Az ushered me into the dancers' dressing room and made the introductions. None of the girls remembered me. Not that I expected anything else. Lucifer had not only gotten to Priyanka, he'd gotten to every single one of them.

I sighed as I joined Pri along the bank of mirrors and picked up a mascara wand. It didn't feel right to be here like this, applying makeup and doing my hair while the fate of the world rested on my shoulders. Surely, there was something more I could do.

Like find that damn memory box.

Unfortunately, Az had made good on his promise. He hadn't let me out of his sight except for bathroom breaks. I'd searched every inch of the toilet, the medicine cabinet, and the shower. If he had the memory box, it wasn't in there.

Although that sure would have made life easier.

"What's wrong, Mia?" Pri asked as she brushed her

long, ebony hair away from her face. "Thought you'd be more excited about your first night working at *Infernal*. It's a great gig. Four hours of dancing and having fun in the club. It's good money, too."

"It's not that." I dropped the mascara back onto the table and turned to her. "Look at me, Priyanka."

Frowning, she turned my way. "What's up?"

"I don't seem at all familiar to you? Not even just a flicker of recognition?"

She scrunched up her face. "Have we met before?"

"Yes," I said insistently. "Hell, we're even friends. You and I got close several weeks back. And then Lucifer got to you and erased all your memories of me."

Her face clouded over. "Az mentioned you might say something like this."

Surprise flickered in my gut. "He did?"

"Yeah, he told me to ignore every word you said." She turned back to the mirror and picked up her brush again. "He seems to think you're untrustworthy."

"Well, fuck." Groaning, I leaned back in my chair and closed my eyes. I hated Lucifer. With every fiber of my being. Even if my past self had been the one to ruin everything, he was the one doing it now. He'd turned my life inside out. Literally. For so long, I'd yearned to be invisible. I hadn't wanted anyone to know my name.

Careful what you wish for.

"Of course, I like to make up my own mind about things," she said, cutting through my dark thoughts.

I flipped open my eyes. "Yeah?"

She blessed me with the best gift I'd received in a very long time. A soft smile and a nod. "What you're saying is crazy. But it's almost so crazy that it can't be a lie. It's like...if you wanted to make something up, you'd pick something way more believable than this. Because if you aren't lying, it means that Lucifer has erased how many memories?"

"Um." I counted. "Six demons. One werewolf lawyer. And six dancers. At a bare minimum. There could be more. Anyone connected to Az who might remember me from before."

"That sounds completely bonkers. How would he have gotten away with it?"

"Because he's a tricky bastard."

"Ha." She nodded. "I'll give you that. But why would he want to erase so many memories of a werewolf girl?"

I winced. "I'm not actually a werewolf. I'm mortal. This is just a scent glamor."

She arched her brows and let out a low whistle. "Didn't see that one coming."

"This is not my hair either." I picked at the brown strands. "I'm a natural redhead, but I got a glamor for it awhile back since it's pretty memorable."

Leaning forward, she searched my eyes. "But why would Lucifer want us to forget about a *mortal*? That's even more bizarre than the werewolf thing, Mia."

"I know something. A lot of things, actually. And he doesn't want me to tell Az about them." I loosed a long, jagged breath. "The thing is, Pri. Lucifer dragged me to Hell, and now he's sent me back here to get to Az. Only I don't want to get to Az. I want to warn him. And he won't listen to a damn word I say."

Her brows shot to the top of her forehead. "You know what the craziest thing is? I think I actually believe you."

My heart lifted. "You do?"

"I mean, I probably shouldn't, but...yeah." She pressed her hand against my knee, squeezing tight. "We're friends, yeah?"

I nodded. "Yeah, Pri. We're friends."

She gave my knee another squeeze. "Then, we need to get Asmodeus to listen to you. And I want to get my fucking memories back."

"You think he'll hear what you have to say about it?"

A strangled laugh popped from her throat. "What do you think?"

"I think he's stubborn as hell, and he's already made up his mind about me," I said with a sigh.

"Exactly. Which is why you need proof."

"Proof," I repeated. While Priyanka turned back to the mirror to finish her makeup, I wracked my brain for proof. The problem was, of course, that Lucifer hadn't left me any. I needed someone Az trusted who also remembered me. But everyone he trusted didn't know me.

There had to be something else. Something I could show him. A token of our past together. If only I'd left my suitcase at his place, I could show him my clothes...

I sat up a little straighter in my chair. Pri glanced over at me with a sly smile.

"You've thought of something."

"Yeah," I whispered, wishing I'd thought of it sooner. With hope in my heart, I patted the ring hidden in the depths of my jean pocket. Surely my having that meant something. "I think I know exactly what to say to him."

*A*fter my shift, Az walked us back home. The night breeze cooled my damp face and curled across my skin like shadows. The club had been jampacked tonight, and I'd searched the crowd for familiar faces who might recognize me. No such luck.

Az was quiet when we strode into his penthouse. He flipped on the lights and passed me a clean pair of pajama shorts and a tank top. Then, he motioned toward the bathroom without a word.

I frowned. "Why are you so grumpy?"

"You were spreading your lies around the club tonight," he said tensely. "It made my dancers start questioning me. Lie to me all you want, Mia, but leave my girls out of this."

Frustration burned through me, and I gripped the pajamas like they were a rope that would drag me out of this new hell and onto the shore of familiarity. Where Az stopped staring at me with hatred in his eyes. I couldn't take this much longer.

"Fine. I won't do that. I've never done that actually." I glared up at him. "Because everything I'm saying is the truth."

He stepped back, holding up his hands. "Just go and change for bed." When I tried to argue, he cut me off. "No. Priyanka said you were going to show me something that would convince me you're telling me the truth, but I don't want to hear any of it, okay? Go change, and go to bed. I won't hear another word from you tonight."

"You're acting like a dick, Az," I said softly.

His jaw rippled with tension. "You're lying to me. If

you knew me as well as you say you do, you'd under-stand why that matters. Loyalty and trust matter more than anything else. I know you believe telling me this story will endear you to me somehow, but what you don't understand is that it's pushing me away."

I blinked, my heart ripping in half. This was why Lucifer had chosen me to do his terrible, wicked deed. Betrayal was the worst sin in Az's eyes. Even from someone he didn't remember.

"Fine." Tears burned my eyes, and I twisted away. "I'll go get changed."

The tank top was soft and delicate against my bare skin, but I barely noticed it. I was too focused on Az's words. The look of hatred in his eyes. This had all gone terribly wrong, and I didn't know what to do about it. Telling him the truth didn't work. Lying to him didn't work. No matter what I said, it was the wrong thing.

And I still didn't know where the memory box was. *Argh!*

I was starting to think I might have to try a different tactic, although I was in deep with this one. As long as Az wouldn't let me out of his sight, I was committed to my failing plan. Find the memory box. Restore Az's memories. But how could I find the thing if I could barely pee in peace?

It was enough to make a girl scream into the void and then sit down with a pizza, a chocolate cake, and a trash reality series on Netflix.

After I showered, I found Az asleep on the floor. Yep, that's right. He had tossed a blanket and pillow onto the floor and sprawled across it, eyes shut to the world. His breathing wasn't steady though, so he was only faking it.

Rolling my eyes, I climbed into the bed and sighed against the silken sheets. Never in my life had I slept in a bed as comfortable as his. So, if he wanted to sulk on the floor, fine with me. I could starfish all night if I wanted.

But sleep never came. I was far too aware of Az's scent, his breath, his steady presence in the room. He was *right there* and yet it felt like he was further away than when I'd been trapped in Hell. I spread my fingers across his pillow and breathed in the scent of fire. But all that did was wind me up, clenching my core with a need that was bordering on criminal.

"I can smell you," he said.

"I don't care," I mumbled into the pillow.

"Can't sleep?"

"At this point, I'm not sure I'll ever sleep again."

"Humans are so dramatic."

My heart pounded my ribs. Human?

"Priyanka told me about your werewolf glamor." He pushed up from the floor and strode toward me. Darkness clung to his skin. "Said you're hiding what you are. Is it because you wanted the job at my supernatural club?"

"I thought you didn't believe a word I said," I snapped.

"Do you want to know why?" Slowly, he eased onto the bed beside me, and his skin brushed mine. My heart nearly stopped.

"I have a pretty good idea," I said around a tight throat. "You don't trust people, especially not strangers. So when a stranger comes in with a wild story about forgotten memories, your first instinct is to think she's some kind of monster trying to take you down."

"I don't think you're a monster," he said softly.

I snorted. "You could have fooled me."

"If you're telling the truth," he said, "it means that Lucifer knows what the Legion and I are doing in Manhattan."

I lifted my head to gaze up at him. "I'm shocked you'd say that to me. Aren't you afraid I'll run off and tell someone you're working against him? Isn't that what this is all about?"

"What are we up to, Mia?" He took my chin in his fingers and pierced my soul with his eyes. "If you know me as well as you say you do, you'll know what we do behind closed doors."

I swallowed hard, so focused on his touch that I almost didn't hear his words. "You're trying to save souls. You don't want Lucifer to win the game, so you're doing whatever you can to stop him. The fewer points he gains, the better."

"Interesting," he murmured. "And I told all this to a mortal?"

"Yeah," I whispered. "We got...close."

"Your desire," he whispered back. "We were lovers."

A shiver went through me at the word, and a new wave of longing washed over me. He widened his eyes, clearly scenting it. Emotions could not be faked. Words could.

"Are you actually...considering what I'm telling you?" I asked, almost too afraid to hope.

"I'll be honest, Mia. I don't want to believe a damn word you're saying. The implications are..."

"Fucked up?"

He chuckled, a familiar rumble that I loved. "Priyanka said you have some proof. I'd like to see it."

"Proof that I know you. Proof that we were once close." Heart in my throat, I climbed out of bed and padded over to my jeans. I pulled the ring out of my pocket and held it up. "You gave me this. So that I could protect myself with its powers."

14

Az leapt from the bed, crossed the room, and took the ring from my shaking hands. I wanted to pull it back to my chest, to keep it with me always. All these weeks spent apart, the ring had kept him close to me. It was a part of him that had always been by my heart.

As mortifyingly cheesy as that sounded.

"This is mine," he breathed, holding it up to his eyes and turning it over in his fingers. "You said I gave this to you?"

"Yeah. It's a really long story that starts with Rafael and ends with Lucifer, but basically, you wanted me to have it so that it could keep me safe."

His brows furrowed when he glanced at me. "But you're mortal. You can't use the power of this ring."

"Turns out I can," I said with a shrug. "When Rafael —oh, it was Michael, actually—backed into a corner alley, I used the ring. It did a blasty thing at him. Then, you showed up with Abaddon and—"

"Wait a minute." His voice turned dark. "Rafael and Michael? You're saying they've gone after you before?"

I pressed my lips together. "Yeah. A few times. We tried to stop them but—"

Az jammed his fingers into his hair, and I fell silent. I was throwing too much information at him. It was far too much to process. Hell, I could *actually* remember it, and I still had trouble with the convoluted mess my life had become.

"This sounds insane."

"You're right," I said, not missing a beat. "It's totally bonkers. I wished it wasn't."

He shook his head and began pacing the length of his room. "If you're right, I can't continue on blindfolded like this. I need my memories back. Otherwise, we're fighting in the dark."

I let out a sigh of relief. The ring had done the trick. Az was actually starting to believe me. Maybe I could pull this off, after all.

"Exactly," I said as a blinding smile filled my face. "And I know how to do it."

He stopped pacing. "How?"

"There's a little black box. The last time I saw it, it was here." I gazed around his room. "I figured you might have found it when I vanished. Maybe you hid it somewhere for safe-keeping."

Light dawned in his eyes. "That's why you keep mentioning the damn box. And that's why Rafael is after it."

"Exactly."

"Fuck." With a growl, he whirled toward the wall and slammed his palm against it. The sound reverberated in my ears, chilling me to the bone. That was not the sound of someone who was excited about having his memories restored.

"Where's the black box, Az?" I whispered.

He sagged against the wall, his chest heaving. "I destroyed it."

My heart shuddered to a stop, and I pressed a hand to my throat. "No."

He couldn't have. I wouldn't let this be the truth. If Az had destroyed the box, my entire plan was more doomed than I'd thought. He'd never get his memories back. Not unless we found another one, but where would we even begin to search for something like that? I swallowed down the scream building in my throat.

"So, when you say you destroyed it, do you mean you just threw it away somewhere? Right?" I bit my lip, wincing when I chomped down too hard from the tension rattling my body.

"No." He moaned and slammed a hand against the wall again. "I turned it to ash when I found it."

My eyes widened. "Why would you do that?"

"I sensed darkness in it when I found it on the floor." He shook his head and pushed away from the wall. "I'd never seen it before, and there it was. I thought it was something destructive, left there by my enemies. And so I got rid of it."

He whirled on me then, his eyes alight with fire. "Maybe this is another lie. Another trick. You have my ring, but how does that prove anything?"

"Ask me anything," I whispered. "What's something only I could know if we were close?"

He stalked toward me, shadows whorling across his face. "What do I hate most in this world?"

"Betrayal."

"Hmm." He narrowed his eyes. "And what do I love the most?"

"The Legion, your family."

Shaking his head, he took a step back. "Those are too easy."

"Ask me something harder." I reached up and wound my hands around his, pulling them down to my beating heart. I wouldn't end this night until he listened to everything I said. Until he looked into my eyes and understood the truth.

"What's the worst thing that has ever happened to me?"

My heart thumped, and I dropped my voice to the softest whisper I could manage. "Losing Morax."

He sighed and closed his eyes. "Who is my greatest enemy?"

I frowned. "That seems like a trick question."

His eyes flipped open. "Answer it."

For a moment, I let my mind spin over his question. It was a trick. He thought I would answer Lucifer. It was what anyone else would say. That or the Creator. But that wasn't the truth. Not really.

"Anyone who threatens your Legion," I finally said.

He swept his gaze across my face as if searching for something. When he spoke, there was something like awe in his voice. "You do know me."

"Better than you can imagine." I squeezed his hands and leaned forward so that our bodies brushed. Sparks of heat stormed across my skin, sending shockwaves of desire through my core.

"So, then what happened?" he murmured. "Why did he erase you from my mind? Where have you been? I'm guessing the reason we had an opening for a dancer was because you're the one who had the job before? We were wondering what happened. No one knew why we were one girl down."

I nodded, swallowing hard. "We were all going after Lucifer. He realized our plan, and then he led you all into the dungeon beneath *Infernal*. When I followed after you, you were already gone. I guess he trapped you somehow and erased your memories. And then he found me and took me straight to Hell."

Az stiffened against me. When he spoke, there was anger in his voice, but it wasn't directed toward me. "He dragged a mortal girl to Hell? Why? What did he want with you? Why did he let you go?"

"It would be a lot easier to explain everything if you had your memories." I sighed, thinking. I'd tell him as much as I could, but I'd leave out the heart rippy thing. Az had finally let down his barriers, but he didn't know me, not like I needed him to. One wrong move, and we'd be back at square one. If he knew I'd signed a deal with the devil to rip out his heart...yep, best not mention that part.

"Just tell me, Mia."

"He wants you dead, Az. The thing he most wants in this world is to see you dead."

"Why?" he growled.

"I guess he sees you as a threat. He thinks you're going to end the game of souls somehow." That much was close enough.

"And so you found your way back to me so you could warn me." He wound his arms around me and pulled me against his chest. My eyes fluttered shut as a heavy sense of calm settled onto my shoulders like a weighted blanket. I'd been carrying around so much tension for days that the knots in my shoulders had formed boulders, and the fiery heat of him was the only thing that could soothe them.

We stood like that for a long time. Twenty minutes, maybe more. So long that my eyelids grew heavy, and for the first time in days, I felt like I could sleep. When Az finally pulled back, there was a softness in his expression I hadn't seen since I'd been dragged into Hell.

"I'll be honest," he said in a soft voice. "I don't know what to make of all this, and I'm not sure what my next move should be. But I do know one thing, Mia. And it's that I felt a connection with you from the moment I set eyes on you."

A shudder went through me, and he smiled.

"I thought maybe you didn't," I whispered. "You have been kind of grouchy with me, you know."

His lips quirked. "Hmm. I could say the same for you."

"I was grouchy because you wouldn't believe a damn word I said."

He cocked a brow. "Would *you* have believed yourself if you were me?"

"Probably not." A light laugh escaped from my parted lips. "In fact, I might have told you to fuck off."

"Good thing I didn't do that, then, eh?" He curled a finger beneath my chin. "Unless that's something you want from me, and based on your scent, I imagine it is."

Swallowing hard, I dropped back my head to gaze up at him. My heart throttled forward like a wild horse. Had I actually heard that right? Or was I misunderstanding him? Surely he wasn't *hitting on me*.

"Oh, is that right, Asmodeus? You want me to fuck

off?" With a sly smile, I pulled out of his arms and tiptoed over to the bedroom door. "Guess I better go sleep in the other room then."

Chuckling, he grabbed my arm and tossed me onto the bed. I bounced on the soft mattress, my breath whooshing out of me. A wicked smile played across his lips as he stalked toward me.

And then he slowly knelt beside the bed.

I gazed down at him with a thumping heart as his deft fingers pushed my t-shirt up around my hips. I hadn't put on the pajama shorts, so all that stood between his mouth and my core was a pair of thin, silky panties.

A low growl rumbled in the back of his throat, pebbling my arms with goosebumps. I'd heard that sound from him before. It took me back to a better time when he knew my name and all my darkest secrets. And accepted me anyway.

My heart yearning for that moment, I wound my fingers through his soft hair and arched toward him. I wanted to feel his mouth on me again. I wanted him to taste me and fuck me and drive me so crazy that I forgot all of the terrible things that had happened to bring us here.

His thumb pressed against my panties, rocking my core. I shuddered at his touch, need roiling through me like a hurricane. He murmured something too low for me to hear, and for a split second, his hand stilled.

"Is this what you want?" he asked, glancing up at me.

The way he knelt between my thighs made it look like he was worshipping the altar of my hips and everything beneath them.

Heart thundering, I nodded. "Of course I do. Can't you tell?"

"What if I'm different?" he murmured. "What if I'm not like the male you know?"

"Az," I breathed. "How could you be any different? The only thing you forgot is me."

"Because forgetting you feels like a sin. So wrong it should be impossible."

I shuddered at his words.

"I wish it was," I whispered. "If I could change anything at all, it would be that."

His thumb brushed against me once more. Pleasure stormed through my core, clenching me. Slowly— agonizingly so—he pushed aside my panties so that there was no longer anything at all between me and him. He lowered his head between my thighs and dragged his tongue across me.

Sparks stormed through my vision. I cried out, fisting the sheets. I clung on like they were a lifeline in a sea of painful pleasure. I needed him so badly I could barely take it. I wanted more. So much that I would never walk the same again.

His tongue speared me, and I shook around him. Fingers digging into my thighs, he flicked and teased and drove me to the edge. In what felt like only seconds, I shattered. All my need rose up like a storm and thundered through me in a climax that left me breathless and unmoored.

My chest heaved as he slowly unwound my legs from his neck. I hadn't even realized I'd clung on to him like that. A wicked smile curved his lips and danger danced in his eyes.

"You really do like it when I touch you." He winked.

"You have no idea," I whispered, swallowing hard when he stood and pushed his pants to his feet.

He was ready for me, his cock hard and throbbing with the same anticipation I felt between my legs. I was ready for him again already. He covered me with his corded body and plunged deep inside. I swallowed down a scream of pleasure as his cock hit my G-spot. My body convulsed; my ears roared.

With a smile, he grabbed my wrists and trapped them on the bed. "I can tell you've been tense." He thrust deeper inside of me. "I'm going to make you come so many times that you forget what that tension feels like."

"Sounds good to me," I breathed.

Az's cock throbbed inside me. He pulled out and thrust inside, harder than each time before. I could barely think straight. I'd been dreaming of this moment, wishing he could see past the stranger and recognize the girl he'd once...cared for.

He was still the same Az. Everything about him was exactly how he had always been. The way he smelled. The way he smiled. The way it felt like our bodies were made for each other.

With a growl, he flipped me over and spanked me hard on the ass. A cry ripped from my throat. He gripped my hips and plunged inside, and a new delicious thrill ran down my spine. This was more than just sex. It was animalistic and raw, like somewhere deep inside of him, he actually recognized me for who I was.

I rocked back against him as his pace quickened. Our bodies slammed together, and my pleasure pulsed harder in my core. I gripped his sheets and let go, giving in to the climax. It rocked through me, even more intense than before. It was all I could do to remember my name when it was over.

Az slammed into me once more, coming just behind me. His roar shook the walls and my soul. Slowly, he pulled out and gave my ass another spank.

Sighing, I slumped against the bed and smiled. My heart still raced in my chest, but my eyelids were so heavy, I could barely keep them open. He'd done as promised. Not a single cell of my body was tense anymore.

"I think I might be able to sleep now."

He chuckled and settled onto the bed beside me. "Not so fast. I want to ravage you, Mia. And I'm only just getting started."

15

I awoke with Az's arms wrapped around my body and my cheek pressed against his corded chest. For a moment, I forgot about everything. Hell had never happened. Lucifer's deal didn't exist. Instead, it was a few weeks back. Az and I had been dancing around our feelings for days. Before we both finally gave into it.

But then my new reality slowly came crawling back into my mind. Lucifer's deal. Az's lost memories. The time ticking by at super speed. Another day was gone, and I still had no idea how I was going to stop Lucifer.

At least Az trusted me now.

Kind of.

Hopefully, it would be enough.

"Good morning," Az murmured with a lazy smile, his eyes shut to the world. His dark lashes flared across his sharp cheekbones, and his nose dipped down to a pair of full lips. The guy was a goddamn masterpiece.

"Morning," I said, feeling a little shy. Even though he

was Az, it was like we were starting things all over again.

"Sleep well?"

"Surprisingly, yes." I flushed. "Might have had something to do with your tongue."

"My tongue and something else, I hope." He flipped onto his side and gazed at me. Unease churned in the depths of his eyes. Despite our lighthearted chat, his mind was locked on what we'd discussed last night. I'd dropped a lot of bombs on him, and now he had to pick up the pieces. At least I was by his side to help him.

"What are we going to do?" I whispered.

He pursed his lips, sighed. "I don't like being in the dark. By erasing all my memories of you, he's erased everything that happened leading up to your disappearance. That's important information, Mia."

"I can go over all of it with you, if you'd like."

"I want my memories back." He threw back the covers and climbed out of bed. Stark naked. I'm not ashamed to admit that I stared. "The Legion needs their memories back. The dancers do, too. He's stolen from us, and I will not let him get away with it." His gaze swept across me. "And I want to remember you, Mia."

My heart swelled. The look in his eyes when he'd opened his door and saw me as a stranger had been one of the worst moments of my life. I had him back now, but it wasn't the same. It would never be the same, no matter how close we got. Not unless he could remember me.

"But how? You destroyed the memory box."

"What do I do when there's a problem?" he asked. Despite everything, Az kept doing this. Asking me questions to see if I had the right answer to give him. I knew there was a part of him that wasn't one hundred percent sure of me. Even now.

"Call a meeting with the Legion."

He nodded. "Get dressed. We'll head to the club after breakfast."

🐚

*T*he Legion listened with wide eyes and dropped jaws. I let Az take the lead and explain as much as he could. Every now and then, one of them would glance my way. Phenex still didn't look convinced, though the cautious curiosity in Caim's eyes was a good sign. Bael and Stolas said little. Valac huddled in the corner staring at me. You know, the usual.

"This sounds like a load of bullshit," Phenex argued, folding his arms and leaning back in his chair. "And a little too convenient, don't you think? How did Lucifer manage to get to all of us?"

"He led you into a trap." I finally spoke up.

"There are six of us and one of him." Phenex's frown deepened. "He's the King of Hell, but we're Princes. No way he would have been able to do it."

"He had a little help, according to Mia." Az turned to me. "Rafael has been working with Lucifer this entire time."

Phenex snorted. "Yeah. Shocker. We already knew that."

"Hey, Valac," Caim called over his shoulder. "What do you reckon? Is Mia telling the truth about all this?"

Oh no. Not this again. I steeled myself as Valac's gaze scraped across my bones. It was like he was carving me inside out, digging deep for the thing that made me who I am. And then gobbling it up, spitting it out, and staring at it like it was pile of prophetic tea leaves.

Or maybe I was just being dramatic.

"She is not a werewolf, so that much is true. I should have seen it before. Mia has a human essence. Kind of." Valac's eerie voice rang in the silence of the room. "And there is truth in her words, though there is something dark in her soul. She is not a normal human."

Great. Thanks, Valac. Couldn't leave that last bit off, now could you?

Phenex laughed. "Something dark? See, I told you she's trouble."

"We all have dark spots on our souls," Az said in a voice that was firm and unyielding. "We won't judge Mia for hers."

My heart thundered in my chest. I hadn't expected him to say something like that. I shifted on the chair, and it creaked beneath my weight. "I probably am trouble, to be honest. Just not the kind you mean."

Phenex grunted. "Maybe I should just feed you to the fishes and make all of this go away."

"Sure, go ahead." I shrugged. "But that won't stop Lucifer from coming after you all."

"Let him come." He pounded his fist against his open palm. "I'm sick and tired of playing games and pretending to be loyal to him. We've been his puppets on strings for far too long. It's time for war."

"Phenex," Stolas piped up from his spot at the table. He was surrounded by piles of ancient books. "What have we said about your temper?"

"You think *this* is my temper?" Phenex pushed up

from the chair and stormed over to the wall. "I'll show you my temper."

"Please don't punch the wall again," I said at the same time Stolas and Bael uttered the very same thing. The ginger's fist fell to his side, his mouth ajar. Stolas and Bael stared.

Caim's grin spread wide. "If she's not one of us, I'll eat Phenex's dirty socks."

Phenex growled, knelt to the floor, and started to pull off his boots. "Go right ahead. I hope you choke on them."

"He's punched walls in front of you before?" Stolas asked, closing the book before him.

"Once. At Valac's place. We were talking about Rafael and Lucifer and all the murders. I don't remember why Phenex got so pissed, but he took it out on the wall."

Valac glanced up, his eyebrows lifted. I think it was the first time I'd ever really seen him surprised. "We wondered how that hole came to be there, but none of us could remember what had happened."

"Well, now you know." I nodded. More proof. What a relief.

"And I'm going to have to punch another wall if we don't get on with this." Phenex redid his laces and dropped back into his chair. He gave me a nod, like he'd accepted what I'd said. But he still didn't look too happy about it. With a grunt, he whirled toward Caim, who still sat there with that goofy smile on his face. "And you need to pipe down."

"I didn't say a damn word." Caim chuckled. "You're just mad because Mia's proven you wrong."

"Fuck off," Phenex said.

"You fuck off."

I couldn't help the smile that took over my face. This was it. Home. The Legion bickering like brothers. Az standing firmly by my side. They didn't remember me, but it didn't matter. We'd still found our way back to each other.

"As riveting as this conversation is," Az cut in, "let's get back to why we're here. Lucifer has stolen our memories as a way to take us down. We need to find a way to restore them so that we can make a solid plan. Any ideas, Stolas?"

Stolas had brought a selection of his ancient texts to the meeting, and he'd spent most of the conversation flipping through the pages. With a sigh, he shook his head. "Nothing so far. There's quite a bit about demons erasing memories, but the texts don't suggest a way to get them back."

Az paced before the gathered demons.

Bael leaned back in his chair, his blonde hair gleaming beneath the overhead fluorescent lights. "Could the fae help?"

Ugh. Not the fae again. I already owed them for a glamor. I didn't want to owe them for something else. That combined with Lucifer's demon deal, and my fate was wound up in too many promises. Another one might just break the camel's back.

"No." Az shook his head. "Fae don't wield that kind of magic, but the witches might. I'll pay them a visit tomorrow."

"Tomorrow?" I shifted on my seat. "We should go today."

Az cut his eyes my way. "Why?"

"Time is running out," I said, though I didn't know

how to say more than that without mentioning the whole heart rippy thing. "Lucifer said he would be here in a week. That was two days ago. We literally don't have the time to waste."

"One more day won't much of a difference," he murmured, turning back to the Legion. "We have to keep up appearances. Act like everything is normal. Lucifer doesn't know you planned to warn us, does he?"

"Yeah, not exactly. If he knew that, he wouldn't have let me go."

He nodded. "So, we can't do anything that will give us away."

"I don't see how going to visit the witches will tip him off," I argued, pushing up from the chair. "We really need to get this sorted out now, Az. The longer we wait, the less likely we are to win."

Az shook his head, sighing. "I've heard a rumor that Eisheth is coming to the club tonight. I assume you know who she is?"

I ground my teeth together. "Unfortunately."

"She's likely spying for Lucifer. If we're not here, she'll know something is up."

"I don't like this," I said, plopping back onto my chair.

"It's just one more night," he said gently. "Let's all go do our jobs and pretend like nothing odd is happening. Is everyone in agreement?"

The demons nodded, and all I could do was sigh. *Here we go again.* More pretending. At least I'd had enough practice by now.

16

That night, I danced like I'd never danced before. I lost myself in the music and let it all out. I'd been running on fumes for days, and bottling up my emotions never turned out well.

As the sweat beaded on my brow, I searched the club for any sign of our VIP guest. I spotted her in the back corner. She was alone, even though she was dressed to the nines, like she was out on a big date. Long red gown that matched her painted lips. Her sleek hair curtained a face that was focused on me. She might be a sociopathic narcissist who sacrificed innocent humans, but at least she looked good doing it.

Her lips curved in the corners when I met her gaze. That was a smile of recognition.

Eisheth *saw* me, for me, which meant Az was partially right. If Lucifer hadn't bothered to wipe her memories, she was probably spying for him. Just like Rafael.

Wonderful.

I decided not to let her get to me. Let her spy. All

she'd see was a girl dancing and trying to get close to the demon she was bound to kill. She watched me for the rest of the night, but she didn't make a move to come any closer.

When my shift was over, I headed to the bathroom while the rest of the girls returned to the dressing room. After four hours in that cage, I always needed a trip to the ladies' room. Desperately so.

As my high heels clicked on the floor, the overhead lights flickered. A chill swept down my arms, and a strange sense of deja vu rushed over me again.

"Hello, Mia," Eisheth said sweetly from behind me.

My heart hammered my ribs. I sucked in a sharp breath and slowly spun on my heels. There she was. My vampire nemesis with her long dark hair and perfectly-fitted dress that hugged her every curve. She'd not only tried to sacrifice my soul to Lucifer, but she'd also ripped out Morax's heart.

My cheeks burned with rage.

"Go away, Eisheth. You shouldn't be back here, and I have nothing to say to you." I started to turn away, but she cleared her throat, stopping me.

"I wouldn't be so dismissive of me if I were you." She shifted closer, sneering into my face. "Lucifer sent me here to make sure you do exactly what he's asked of you."

"Yeah, I figured that out myself, thanks." Rolling my eyes, I tried to step past her, but she dodged to the side. "Can you please get out of my way?"

"Why haven't you done it yet?" she hissed. "Instead of fulfilling your end of the deal, you're back dancing in that fucking cage."

"Yeah. To convince Az he can trust me." I folded my

arms, hoping to drown out my fear with my irritation. I couldn't let her realize exactly how I felt. "I already explained all this to Rafael, and hovering is the exact opposite of helping. What if Az caught me talking to you?"

She chuckled. "He'd never kill you. He's far too soft for that."

"Maybe not. But he'd definitely kick me out of here and never let me speak to him or his Legion again. How am I supposed to get close enough to rip out his heart that way?"

"Stop stalling, Mia," she said with an exaggerated eye roll. "You're close enough to him *now*. He's let you into his inner circle. It's time to rip the bandaid off. Seduce him and kill him. Before time runs out."

Narrowing my eyes, I stepped in close. "Why are you so invested in this anyway? You know what happens if I pull this off, right? Lucifer ends the game of souls. I didn't think you'd want that."

"It means the Creator doesn't win. As far as I can tell, that's good for everyone. Including you, Mia McNally."

"Go away, Eisheth. Before someone catches me talking to you."

"Hmm." She tsked and tapped my forehead. "Fine. I'll make myself scarce. But I'll be watching you."

Eisheth vanished around the corner, and I slumped against the wall. Lucifer *really* didn't believe I'd carry out my part of the plan. Otherwise, he wouldn't keep sending spies to berate me about it. Az had been right. Lucifer was watching me so closely that we couldn't risk making the wrong move. Right now, he thought I was dragging my feet, but he didn't know that I'd spilled the beans. I couldn't do anything that would make him think I had.

Two black boots stepped into my view. I lifted my head to find Valac before me, leaning against the wall with arms crossed.

"That was an enlightening conversation," he said softly.

Alarm jolted my heart. I cast a glance behind me, thankful that no one else was there. But...this wasn't good. Had he heard everything Eisheth and I had said?

"I don't know what you mean," I said slowly. Maybe if I pretended we'd had a normal conversation, he'd ignore his ears and go away. *Ha!*

"Nice try." He shook his head. "I heard everything. It seems you've left out a few important details. I'd say I'm surprised, but I'm not. I sensed something else inside you, Mia. I knew it was there. Unfortunately, it's turned out to be far worse than I thought."

"Valac," I whispered, all the blood draining out of my face. "It's not what it sounds like."

He lifted his brows. "Oh? What's it like then?"

"Some of what you heard is true. I did make a deal with Lucifer."

"To rip out Az's heart."

I swallowed hard. "Yes, to rip out Az's heart. But he didn't give me any other choice. If I didn't sign his damn demon contract, he was never going to let me leave Hell."

"I fail to see how that makes any of this okay," he argued. "You're willing to rip out Az's heart just so you can be free? And here I thought you cared deeply for him."

"I do care for him, Valac." I fisted my hands, blinking

back the tears. "Which is why I have no intention of fulfilling my end of the deal. I just signed it so I could get out of there. I'm not going to do it. I'd rather lose my soul."

Valac slid his gaze across my face. "Hmm. That feels like the truth. So, why didn't you tell Az about it?"

"Think about how it sounds," I whispered back. "He doesn't know me. He barely trusts me. If I tell him Lucifer sent me here to rip out his heart, how do you think he's going to react?"

"I'm not sure, but I'm afraid you're going to have to find out." He held up his hands when I started to argue. "I'll give you a chance to do it the way you want to. See if the witches can find a way to unlock his memories. If they can't help him, you have to come clean. Az was right about what he said earlier. We'll never win against Lucifer unless we have all the information we can get. That includes the real reason he sent you here."

"I can't help him if he pushes me away, Valac."

"So, you'll just have to hope the witches have the answers you need." Valac jerked up his head, and his eyes went black. "Az is coming. I'll cover for you tonight, but after that, you're on your own."

17

Valac vanished just before Az rounded the corner. I was still standing there, mind racing, when he strode toward me with purposeful steps. There was a tension in his jaw and fire in his eyes. Uh oh. I'd seen that look. He was mad.

"What are you doing here lurking in the hallway?" he asked, his voice tense. He'd gone back to his grumpy self, it seemed. Gone was the desire in his eyes and the passion in his touch. Mr. Scowly had come out to play.

"I'd hardly say I'm lurking, Az."

"I saw Eisheth follow you back here. Were you talking to her?" he demanded.

Oh, so that was what this was about. At least he hadn't overheard our conversation. He might pull a Phenex if he had.

"Yeah, I was talking to Eisheth. I told you I'd met her in the Before Times," I said. "You know, when you had your memories."

His eyes narrowed. "Don't tell me she's some kind of friend."

"Friend?" I laughed. "Az, she tried to get you to sacrifice my soul."

He blinked and took a step back. "I'd never do such a thing."

"Of course you wouldn't. But she tried all the same. Luckily for my life and my soul, you didn't let her win."

Az slung his hands into his pockets and rocked back on his heels. "Why did she want to talk to you tonight if you're not friendly?"

"Unfortunately for me, she's one of the few supernaturals who actually knows who I am. Lucifer has her poking around to see what we're up to. She's his spy." I sighed. "So, you were right. We need to keep up appearances for awhile."

He leaned forward and fingered a stray strand of my hair. "You've been through a lot with us. Haven't you, Mia?"

I sighed and closed my eyes. "Honestly? You have no idea. I joined your dancers only a couple of months ago, but it feels like way longer than that. It seems like years."

His hand slid around the back of my neck as he breathed me in. Shivers stormed across every inch of my skin, and my back arched instinctively. Desperate need poked up its head, trying to distract me from everything else. It worked.

I didn't really care about Eisheth anymore, not when Az was touching me like this. Like he was two seconds away from ripping off my clothes and plunging himself inside of me. I almost moaned from the image of it in my head.

"This turns you on, does it?" His grip on my neck tightened. I let out a sharp cry and dropped back my head, exposing my skin to him. His lips against me were all I needed now. Otherwise, I'd probably explode.

"Everything you do turns me on," I whispered.

"Now that," he said in a delicious growl, "is definitely a lie. You don't like it when I lock you up in my penthouse and throw away the key."

"Eh." I shuddered when his tongue drifted across my neck. "Depends on why you're locking me up. If it's for *activities*, then chain me, spank me, and trap me all you want. I'm yours."

The words were out of my mouth before I could stop them. For a moment, I'd forgotten about Lucifer's plot to keep us apart. This was the most I'd spoken to the 'new' Az about my feelings, even feelings that focused on sex. I'd tried to keep my cards as close to my chest as I could. But he'd knocked down so many walls that I had no hope of rebuilding them.

"You're mine, are you?" Smiling against my skin, he dragged his lips across my throat. I shuddered and wound my hands around his shirt, clinging on as tightly as I could. "Oh, how I wish I could remember everything I've ever done to you. But I can't. Not yet, anyway. Describe it to me, Mia."

I wet my lips, flushing. Oh. Okay. This was what we were doing now? No complaints from me.

"Well, there was one time you took me to a party." I gasped as his lips drifted further south. "We were in this packed room with lots of supernaturals, and you wanted everyone to think we were an item."

He pulled back, frowning. "So, we weren't an item?"

"At that point, no. We were just pretending. So you could get an invite to the Covenant Ball."

Nodding, he pushed me back against the wall and

braced my hands on either side of my head. I gasped. "Funnily enough, this is exactly what you did at that party. We went into a hallway, there were people all around us, and you..."

"Go on," he purred against my ear.

"My dress was short," I whispered. "So, you decided to drive me crazy with your finger."

"Is that so?" He smiled against my skin and slowly slid his fingers down the length of my body. I couldn't help but tremble from his touch, and he knew it. "Perhaps we should relive it. See if it sparks my memory."

"Yeah, I mean." I gasped when his finger drifted up the inside of my thigh. "That's the best idea I've ever heard in my life. I should have thought of it sooner."

His laughter rumbled against me. My pulse quickened as he pushed his finger beneath my panties and slid inside of me.

Oh my god.

I dropped my head against the wall and widened my legs, desperate for him.

"Was it like this?" he murmured.

"Oh yes."

He slid his finger deeper inside of me, and I gasped. "What now? What did I do to you next, Mia?"

A little of the passion died. I swallowed hard, thinking back to that day. After a little teasing, we'd argued. The outburst had been for show, but I'd meant every word I'd said. I'd wanted him more than I'd wanted to admit, but it felt like he was hot one minute and cold the next. So, I'd shouted at him and stormed out of the party.

That wasn't what I wanted to happen now.

"Nothing came next," I admitted. "We were just

putting on a show for your supernatural friends, and that's all there was to it."

"Ah." His finger stilled, though it stayed inside of me. "A shame, really. I was hoping there was more to it than that. *Much* more to it."

"Fuck me," I whispered.

He growled in response, tightening his grip on me.

"I want you, Az." I arched my back, angling my hips toward him. "And I don't care who sees us."

Az fumbled with his jeans, and he was inside of me before I could even brace myself against the wall. He slammed into me with fiery need in his eyes, his entire body trembling with pent-up power.

I gasped and wrapped my legs around his waist. He plunged inside me once more, quick and hard and rough.

That was when Eisheth rounded the corner again.

She chuckled when she took in the sight of me and Az tangled up together in the middle of a hallway where anyone could pass by at any moment. Irritation flickered in my heart. I *really* didn't appreciate being interrupted like this.

"Whoops." She giggled. "Looks like you two are busy. Or were you *hoping* someone would see you? Demons do have their kinks."

"Go away, Eisheth," Az growled.

"I mean, that *must* be the case, right?" she continued as if he hadn't said a word. "Otherwise, why would you be fucking in the middle of the hallway? You do realize your Legion is right around the corner, yes? Caim, specifically."

I arched my brows, but I didn't say a word. I didn't

want to give her the satisfaction. But Az must have known Caim was nearby. He would have heard him.

Slowly, Az pulled out and zipped up his jeans. I yanked down my dress and tried to pretend my face wasn't ten shades of red. This was pretty mortifying.

"What do you want?" Az asked.

"How is work going?" She smiled when Az narrowed his eyes. "I mean, your corrupting souls work, of course. Not the work of running this club. No one really cares about that, and I'm surprised you actually do. You're a demon, Az. You have better things to do than entertain a bunch of lowly supernaturals."

"You're a lowly supernatural, Eisheth," he said flatly. "As much as you wish you were a demon, you're not. You're just a vamp."

She clucked her tongue. "Well, I've got my eye on you and so does Lucifer. Your contract numbers have been abysmally low lately. If you want to pull your weight, you're going to have to pick up the pace."

So, she was pretending she wasn't here to spy on me. Another game. An annoying one, at that. But if that was how she wanted to play things, fine with me.

"My pace is just fine, Eisheth. You can tell Lucifer I said exactly that." He turned to go, but she clucked her tongue once more.

"Sure thing, Az. Whatever you say. But remember, I'll be watching you."

18

"Come on, Mia." Az threw the covers off my body and pulled me out of bed. I blinked at him through blurry eyes, trying to make sense of what he'd just said. My lids were so heavy, I swore they were attached to fifty pound weights, and the darkness of his room was as thick as midnight.

"What's going on" I mumbled as I rubbed my eyes.

"I realized you were right." He shoved my jeans into my hands. "The longer we wait, the worse this will be. We're going to visit the witches tonight."

His words shot through me like a dose of caffeine. "Wait, tonight? Like right now? What time is it?"

"It's a little after four."

I blinked up at him. We'd gotten home a little after three, and I'd taken ten minutes to get ready for sleep. So, I'd been in bed for all of forty minutes.

He pulled a dark hoodie over his head and grabbed a pair of black shoes from the rack. As he laced them up, he frowned up at me. "Aren't you going to get dressed?"

"You woke me up in the middle of the night to go visit some witches."

"Would you rather we wait until tomorrow?"

"Not really." I hastily blinked the sleep out of my eyes and changed into some normal clothes. Jeans, a dark cropped tee, and my ever-present pair of black boots. "Where did this come from? I thought you were worried about Lucifer's spies."

"It's the middle of the night. They're probably sleeping, other than Eisheth. And she'll be out hunting instead. I saw the look in her eyes tonight. She's hungry."

"Fantastic. Should we bring some stakes with us just in case? We can stab her in the heart if she tries to spy on us."

Az stilled, and he spoke in a voice I'd never heard from him before. "Absolutely not. Eisheth can never be touched. She's the only one in this godforsaken world who knows where Morax is."

Chills consumed me. I'd almost forgotten she was the key to Morax's location. It was why Az had never gotten his revenge for what she'd done. As long as Morax was gone, Asmodeus would never go after her. And she knew it.

It was why she'd had her memories erased. If she couldn't remember where she hid Morax's heart, the Legion could never force it out of her. It was the ultimate insurance policy.

I tugged on my heavy black boots. "Maybe if we find a way to restore your memories, we can do it to her as well. Find out where Morax is after all these years."

Az's body trembled as he slowly stood. "I'm so sorry for ever doubting you, Mia."

My heart thumped. "Don't be. How were you supposed to know that I wasn't just saying all this to get close to you? Lucifer took your memories for a reason. He thought it would keep us apart."

His eyes gleamed with anger, and his lips curled into a wicked smile. "And the tricky bastard didn't win this game."

"Now, we just need to make sure he doesn't win the next one."

Az's smile vanished. "The memories are only part of it. Even if we remember everything, we still won't have a plan to stop him."

I nodded. "Which is why I'm glad we're going to the witches now. The sooner we can restore your memories of everything that's happened, the sooner we can deal with the threat. Otherwise..."

"Otherwise what?"

I shifted on my feet. He wouldn't like what I had to say. I didn't like it much either. "Otherwise, we might have to make a plan without your memories. There's not much time, Az. It's starting to feel like we're focusing on the wrong thing. Lucifer is the threat, regardless of whether or not you can remember it."

"I don't like it." He frowned.

He didn't know about the demon deal. Maybe I should just tell him and fuck the consequences. I closed my eyes. Not yet. We needed to see if the witches could restore his memories first. If they couldn't, then I'd take the plunge and tell him about the deal.

It would be my Hail Mary. Hopefully, I wouldn't need to use it.

"Interesting." Az wound his hand around the back of

my neck and peered into my eyes. "You feel guilty about something."

Ugh. I hated that he could do that.

"I feel a lot of things right now, Az. This situation is kind of crazy, if you haven't noticed."

"But why the guilt?" he murmured, his thumb caressing my throat. I shuddered.

"I don't know. Maybe because it feels like all of this is my fault," I whispered.

Because it was. Kind of. My past self had really screwed things up for Present Me. If only she'd left things alone, the world might not be so fucked. She'd pissed off the King of Hell, and now he was taking it out on me. And the rest of humanity.

"How could any of this possibly be your fault?" Az murmured.

"I made some dumb mistakes," I whispered back. "Which led to Lucifer catching me. If I'd been smarter, he might not have ever gotten his hands on me."

"But I'm the one he wants to kill," Az said with a frown. "What does that have to do with him catching you?"

"Because he's clearly trying to use me against you." I stepped back, pulling out of his embrace before he dug much further. There were too many questions he could ask that would trip me up, and I didn't want to go into the whole demon deal thing until we'd had a chance to visit the witches.

"You know I can still sense you're hiding things from me, Mia," he warned.

"I know." I tried to give him a confident smile, but it came out flat. "There are some things I need to tell you, but you'd understand them far better with your memories intact."

He shook his head. "I knew it."

"How about this?" I said. "I'll make you a promise. As soon as the witches restore your memories, I'll tell you everything."

"Hmm. And why should I agree to that?"

I took his hands in mine and squeezed. "Because you trust me."

After a long moment, he finally nodded. "Alright then, Mia. I'll trust you."

❀

*A*z and I took his personal car uptown to the brownstones lining Central Park. It was quieter up here on the residential streets where picture-perfect walkups were hidden amongst rows of towering trees. We climbed out of the car just outside of a dark red building. The paint was like a splash of blood, standing out from the rest of the brown homes.

We strode up the small flight of stairs, and Az pressed the buzzer.

"On a scale from one to ten, how pissed off are they going to be that we're ringing their bell at four in the morning?"

"Eleven," Az said with a smile.

"Great. That will definitely convince them to help us."

"Good thing they like money."

Ah, of course. Az was depending on the green stuff to get what we needed. I took in the apartment building with new eyes. We were in an expensive part of town,

151

though that could be said for most corners of New York City these days. It was a quiet, residential street that backed up on Central Park. You'd need some serious cash to afford a place like this.

"Are most supernaturals this rich?" I asked him.

"Witches aren't supernaturals. They're humans who have found ways to manipulate the natural order of the world. They're not immortal. They don't have enhanced senses. They require certain herbs and objects and words, as well as years of study. Once they join an Order, they practice until they can venture out on their own. It's a long and complicated process."

"Oh," I said. "So then how can they afford a place like this?"

"The witches provide services that are in high demand. They have more potential clients than they can take on, which means they keep hiking up their prices. As you can see, it works out well for them."

"No kidding," I muttered. Maybe I'd found the wrong calling. Dancing would never make me this kind of money, not even working for Az. "Anyone can become a witch then?"

His brows arched. "If they have a natural inclination for it, then yes. It's like any gift, I suppose." And then he frowned, turning back to the door. "They're taking a long time to wake up."

Sighing, I pushed the buzzer again. "Or they're ignoring us on purpose. If someone rang my bell in the middle of the damn night, I'd pull my covers over my head and curse them with eternal bad breath or something. Maybe turn them into toads while I was at it."

"Probably best you don't take witch classes then," he said with a smile.

We fell silent as we waited. I tapped the concrete with my boots, folding my arms. This really was taking an exorbitant amount of time. Did we need to start banging on the door to wake them up?

Shrugging, I lifted my fisted hand. Az caught my arm, shaking his head.

"Something isn't right," he said in a low voice. "They should have answered by now."

A block of ice slid down my spine. "It's four in the morning, Az. Makes total sense to me."

"There are thirteen witches living in this building," he murmured as he released his grip on my arm. "We would have woken at least one of them."

"Thirteen," I repeated. "Don't tell me that's on purpose."

"It is absolutely on purpose. Thirteen is their lucky number." He inched closer to the door and pressed his ear against the dark wood. After a moment, he shook his head. "Silence. I don't even hear breathing."

Dread churned my stomach, twisting it into knots. "Are your enhanced senses that good?"

"The city is loud, so sometimes it's difficult to hear a mortal's breath. But this is a quiet street. I should be able to hear at least a few of them."

Heart thumping, I tried not to imagine the worst. "But what the hell does that mean? They aren't in there?"

He pressed his lips together. "No, Mia. I don't believe they are."

"Maybe they had another job," I said quickly. "They had to go do a seance or something."

"Perhaps." But Az didn't sound convinced. With a

deep breath, he twisted the knob and pushed the door open. It wasn't locked.

It swung wide, creaking on its hinges. My bones quaked when Az stepped over the threshold and vanished into the shadows of the silent building. I shifted on my feet, pretty sure this was a terrible idea. The last time I'd ventured into a creepy-ass place, I'd ended up dragged through a fiery gate into Hell.

My spidey senses were tingling. And they were telling me to run.

But I couldn't leave Az here to face this alone. Whatever *this* was.

Hopefully, it wasn't another one of Lucifer's traps.

"Az," I hissed as I minced into the building. The door swung shut behind me, slamming hard against the street lamps illuminating the night. Darkness swallowed me whole, making it impossible to see anything. "Az."

"Stay back, Mia," he said, his voice full of barely-contained anger.

My feet slowed to a stop, my heart in my throat. "What is it? What's happened?"

"Someone has already been here," he said quietly. A moment later, he was by my side. "Stay here. I'm going to grab the grimoires, and then we need to leave. And don't touch a damn thing."

Hands shaking, I grabbed his arm when he turned away. "Az, you're freaking me out."

"They're all dead, Mia. Someone slaughtered them. A vampire."

Az left me standing in the center of the entryway, my hands shaking by my sides. They were all dead. Every last one of them. The only ones who might know how to restore the Legion's memories.

Eisheth had been here, but Lucifer was the one behind this. They were doing everything they could to keep Az from remembering. Did they know I'd told him? Or was this insurance in case I did?

Either way, it ended with thirteen slaughtered innocents. Lucifer liked to think he was the hero of his own tale, but he truly was the villain. And I was more determined than ever to take him down.

19

Az's body simmered with anger. He shouted at the driver to return the car to the garage without us, wound his arm around my waist, and launched into the sky. I buried my face in his chest and clung on to his neck, wishing there was something I could say to calm him down.

He was hurting. Az had known these witches. He'd clearly cared about them, more than I'd realized. Lucifer had taken his knife and dug it in a little deeper, piercing Az's heart.

When we returned to his penthouse, the others were waiting for us, along with Priyanka, Serena, and a dozen pizzas. Az didn't say a word to anyone when he released me and vanished into his bedroom in a cloud of pulsing shadows.

I stood there in the middle of his floor, feeling as awkward as hell. Serena met my eyes, and she cocked her head. It felt like I hadn't seen her in five million years, and yet she looked just as badass as always. Even in the middle of the night, she looked calm, collected, and put together.

She wore a smooth grey suit with spiky heels, and her wavy dark hair hung in loose waves around her face.

I opened my mouth to say something to her, but Phenex interrupted me.

"What's happened?" he asked with a frown. "We got a call from Az to meet him here immediately. He sounded panicked, which isn't like him at all."

"He wanted to go to the witches tonight." My eyes drifted toward his open bedroom door. I didn't know how well the demons knew the witches. If they were friends, I shouldn't be the one to share the news. "Az thought it would be better to go while it's still dark."

I should probably go to him. He was clearly hurting. Right now wasn't a great time for him to be alone with his thoughts.

"Oh." Stolas strode over to the coffee table where Az had dropped the books. "Are these grimoires?"

"Yeah," I said slowly. "Az was hoping we'd find a spell in there or something."

Understanding settled in the depths of Stolas's eyes. "Something's happened. Az wouldn't just take a witch's grimoire. And they would never give them up willingly."

I nodded, swallowing hard. "I'm afraid it looked like someone got there before we did. Someone who didn't want us to find a way to restore your memories. So they..."

"Took care of the problem," Phenex grunted before storming away to Az's room. He vanished inside, sucking all the energy out of the penthouse.

"Is that true, Mia?" Stolas asked quietly. "The witches are dead?"

I closed my eyes. "I'm so sorry."

"Hey." Caim crossed the room and gently took my shoulders in his warm hands. "It's not your fault. Don't blame yourself for this."

I trembled at the softness in his voice. Little did he know, it really was all my fault. "If it wasn't for me, Eisheth wouldn't have targeted those witches. She must have realized we'd go there to get a memory restoration spell. So, you're wrong, Caim. It really is all my fault. Those witches are dead because of me."

It was the truth. The horrible, twisted truth. In my efforts to fix things, I'd only made them worse.

"Well, I'm not going to let you blame yourself for this," Caim said firmly. "You're not the bad guy here, Mia. Lucifer is. He's the one trying to take us down, and he's the one we have to aim our anger at. Not you. Alright?"

Tears spilling down my cheeks, I sniffed and gave him a weak nod. He patted me on the shoulder and nodded. "Go see Az. He might need you right now. We'll start looking through the grimoires."

"Alright," I whispered.

As I passed Serena on my way to Az's room, I gave her a slight smile. She flicked her eyes across me, but there was no recognition there. Just curiosity, the kind you gave someone you passed on the street who had a cat sitting on their head.

I hadn't mentioned Serena to the Legion, but I wasn't surprised that she was here. She and Pri had obviously struck up a friendship in my absence. Good.

She gently touched my elbow as I turned away. "Sorry. I have to ask. Do I know you?"

"Yeah, Serena," I said with a sad smile. "You know me."

She winced. "Sorry. I don't remember."

"None of it?" I asked.

She shook her head. Even though I'd expected it, the pain was almost blinding. This was, by far, the worst of it. I'd known Serena all my life. We'd grown up together and had lived side by side. I'd helped her through her shifts. She'd helped me through my trial. Our lives were so wrapped up together that it seemed impossible that Lucifer could fully erase her memories of me.

And yet, somehow, he'd done it.

The fucking bastard.

"Do you remember who lived next door to you when you were a kid?" I couldn't help but ask. "The girl with red hair and—"

Her eyes widened. "And framed ballet slippers on her wall. That was you?"

"Wait." I leaned forward excitedly. "So you do remember?"

"I mean, kind of." Frustration furrowed her brows. "I remember my next door neighbor, but I can't see her face or hear her name. All I know is she was a very big part of my life, and then we drifted apart."

"We never drifted apart."

Her face hardened. "Lucifer did this to me. Didn't he? That bastard. We have to find a way to undo this."

It wasn't the only thing we needed to do, but it was a step in the right direction. I showed her to the grimoires where the others had already begun their research. Phenex trailed out of Az's room, joining them. I took a deep breath and went in.

Az stood before the windows with the curtains flung

wide open. His hands were slung into his pockets, and his shoulders were relaxed. But I knew it was nothing more than an illusion. Inside, rage roared like a lion on the prowl.

"I'm sorry, Az." I stepped up beside him. "Lucifer is..."

"Dead," he growled. When I glanced up at him, he sighed. "At least, he will be once I get my hands on him."

"You can't kill him, I'm afraid," I whispered.

"What?" He frowned. "Why the hell not? Don't tell me you want us to spare his life after everything he's done. *Especially* after tonight."

"The game of souls," I said. "If you kill him, the Creator wins, and this world ends. We have to stop him another way."

Az stepped back. The intensity in his eyes almost knocked me off my feet. "Wait. Are you telling me you know how to stop the fucking game?"

"Yeah," I said, swallowing hard. "I told you I'd tell you everything, and this is part of it. Ripping out his heart will end the game, but I think we both know that's not exactly a good thing."

"Hmm. *I* know that. I've been to the outskirts of the icy plains." He tucked his finger beneath my chin. "But how do *you* know it?"

"Lucifer told me everything when he took me to Hell," I said. "The thing is, it's also true in reverse. Rip out the Creator's heart, and Hell wins."

He grunted. "That's not any better."

"No." I sighed. "It's not. I don't want this world to go to the afterlife, Az. Either of them. But I don't know how we can avoid it."

161

"It's tempting," he mused. "I could rip out his bloody heart and end this once and for all."

"But the ice," I said.

"But the ice." He closed his eyes and pressed his forehead against the glass. "Lucifer has been ahead in the soul game for decades. That's why I've tried so hard to keep his numbers down. But the Creator winning isn't any better. The world is doomed no matter who wins."

I furrowed my brows. "Lucifer is ahead?"

"Yeah." He pushed away from the window and let out a harsh laugh. "Turns out, it's far easier to sacrifice souls to Hell than it is to save them."

"That's odd." I nibbled at my bottom lip. "I could have sworn Lucifer said he's losing right now."

"I've seen the tally myself. You can't trust anything that bastard says, Mia."

No, I couldn't. He was the literal devil. The King of Hell. And yet, I'd lapped it all up. Everything single thing he'd told me. If he'd lied about his numbers, what else had he lied about?

Unease twisted my gut. "I think we need to be very careful about what we do next. Lucifer is playing a game with us, and I don't think we're winning."

"You're right." He wrapped his arms around me and tugged me to his chest. The scent of fire consumed me. "Everything we do from now on, we need to think two steps ahead. Just like he would."

20

We'd been reading the books for hours, and we still didn't have a lead. I'd settled in at the dining table with Hendrix and a bowl of cereal, poring over one of the thickest volumes. Stolas sat opposite to me while Caim hunkered down on my left. The rest of the Legion were huddled in the living room, chowing down on cold pizza.

There was something so achingly familiar about this. If we weren't five days away from total annihilation, I'd probably be pretty happy.

"How's that book looking, Mia?" Stolas asked, glancing up from his dusty book. The ancient parchment crackled in his hands. One wrong move, and that thing would turn to ash.

"There's a lot of weird stuff in here, I've got to admit," I said, wrinkling my nose. It turned out that demons weren't the only ones who were fans of sacrifice. Witches gathered blood and burned it to do a variety of different things, depending on how the blood was kept. Speak to the dead, create an illusion of invisibility, or transform an object into something else. It was pretty advanced stuff.

Impressive, if some of it wasn't creepy as hell.

For example, if the moon and the stars aligned just right, they could bring someone back from the dead. They wouldn't have a soul though. I wrinkled my nose. *No, thank you.* Sounded way too much like a zombie for my liking.

"You must have found one of the dark magic grimoires," Stolas said, nodding. "Not all witches will dabble in that kind of magic. It can take a lot out of them if they aren't careful."

"Sure," I said, like all of this was totally normal. Witches and dark magic spells, dead things without souls, demons who had become my best friends. "So, the memory thing probably isn't in this one then. Unless you consider that dark magic? I don't really know how all this works."

"It depends," he countered. "What spell are you currently reading about?"

"Oh, this one?" I waved at the book and laughed. "Would you believe me if I told you that witches can make zombies? They can bring back dead things and turn them into soulless monsters."

Stolas cocked his head and held out his hand. "Let me see."

I passed him the book. Gladly. I needed to find another grimoire to read. Something as pleasant as a memory restoration spell was about as far from zombie resurrection as one could get.

I pushed up from the table, grabbed another volume from the stack of books, and then returned to my spot

164

across from Stolas. By the time I sat back down, he'd had a good look at the dark magic page.

"I don't think this means what you think it means," he said when I flipped open the leather cover of my next read. "This doesn't make a zombie in the way you're imagining." He shoved a finger at the spell. "It's not like what you've watched on *The Walking Dead*. These beings just have no souls, so they have no morals, no conscience. But it's not like they'd ramble around frothing at the mouth. They'd act pretty normal in fact."

"Can one of those help us get your memories back?" I asked him pointedly.

His shoulders dropped. "You're right. I'm getting distracted like I always do. It's just so interesting..."

He trailed off as he returned to the zombie book. With an amused smile, I dug into my next volume. This one was a lot more promising. Less creepy undead things and more useful spells. Like how to get an object to levitate off the ground.

The hours ticked by. The sun rose and set, bringing the end of another day along with it. I'd read through two more grimoires without finding a damn thing, and I was starting to think this whole plan was pointless. Maybe the witches didn't know how to restore memories. Maybe that black box had been the only thing in the entire world that could do it.

Or maybe I was just being pessimistic.

"I found something!" Serena shouted and leapt from her chair. She waved one of the slimmer volumes, the pages rattling like bones. "I've got it, guys. I've actually got it. This says exactly what we need to do to get our memories back."

My heart leapt into my throat, but I found myself frozen in place. It almost felt too good to be true.

Az stormed across the room and took the book from Serena. He scanned the page with furrowed brows. I expected him to maybe punch the air or something, even though Asmodeus, the First Prince of Hell, would never do that. Still, the tension on his face was unexpected.

"It says it will reveal what is unknown," he said with a frown. "Not that it will restore memories."

Serena's blinding smile whispered away. "That's the same thing, isn't it? Our memories are unknown."

Stolas pushed up from his chair. "It's definitely open to interpretation, but it's the most promising spell we've found."

"Does it say we need to create a little black box or something? That's how the other one was done," I tried.

Serena shook her head. "No, it didn't say anything about that."

She sat hard, and the others who had jumped to their feet followed. A second ago, the excitement had been electric. Now, everyone looked like they'd lost their puppy.

"Maybe we should try it," Stolas said. "A lot of the spells have been vague like that. Perhaps it all depends on your intentions. Focus on an unknown, and that is the thing that will be made known."

"So, what is it we have to do, anyway?" Bael asked, leaning back in his chair.

"Wait for midnight," Serena whispered. "Burn some blood. *Our* blood."

Lovely. Of course it couldn't be anything else.

Az nodded. "Good. I'll shut the club for the night,

and we'll wait here until the clock strikes twelve. No one is to leave in case Rafael or Eisheth are watching the streets. Tonight, the truth will finally be revealed."

"Twenty minutes to go." Az paced in front of where we'd gathered in the living space. He'd dimmed the lights and closed the curtains, just in case Rafael decided to swoop by. If he knew what we were trying to do, he'd do everything in his power to stop us. And then go rat us out to Lucifer.

Az passed everyone a small knife and a coffee mug. The coffee mug was to hold the blood until we burned it. Apparently, this spell required ceramics.

When he reached me, he pressed the weapon into my hands with a knowing glint in his eye.

"Wait. I don't need to do the blood burning thing," I told him. "I haven't lost any memories."

But that wasn't the *full* truth. Most of my past life was nothing more than meaningless blurry shadows. I'd found those moments that Az and I had spent side by side, but nothing else. Centuries of a life, forgotten. This was my chance to remember it all, even if I didn't like what I saw.

"I want you to do it with us," he said firmly. "Just in

case. You wouldn't know if he'd erased anything, would you?"

He had a point. If it wasn't for me, Az and his Legion would still be going about their daily lives, completely unaware of the holes in their minds. Could Lucifer have done the same to me? He'd certainly had ample opportunity when I'd been in Hell, and I wouldn't put it past him.

"Okay, fine." I took the knife and placed it on the hardwood floor in front of me. "I'll do it."

"Good. I'd like you to go first."

"Az." I frowned. "Don't you think it's far more important for *you* to go first? You're the one he wants to kill. And you're the one who might be able to figure out how to stop him."

"I want you to go first." He smile was tense. "Is that a problem?"

My heart hammered my ribs. He still didn't fully trust me.

"Fine," I said through gritted teeth. "If you'll agree to go right after me."

"I wouldn't have it any other way." He smiled.

I frowned as I watched him trail toward the bar and pour himself a drink. Valac edged down beside me and sat cross-legged on my right. He leaned in close, and his bleached hair fell into his eyes. "You didn't tell him."

I hugged my knees to my chest. "No. Not all of it."

"He's going to find out tonight. You do know that, yes? This spell will reveal far more than just our memories."

I'd suspected as much, which was why I hadn't been keen to go first. The wording of the spell was so vague that it could mean anything, and it probably did. Memories and secrets combined. "That's why you need to convince him to burn his blood after I do, regardless of what happens. I don't want him to back out when he hears everything I've done."

"I can't control what Az does, and I think you know that," he whispered.

"Sure, but you're Valac." I smiled up at him. "He knows you can see the truth in people's minds. And if you tell him to go through with it, he'll trust you."

Valac's hollow eyes swept across my face. "You've been nice to me. Most people don't like me very much, you know."

"Everyone has something to hide. And you threaten their secrets. Plus, it does feel kind of weird when you do your soul searching thing."

A smile lifted the corners of his lips. "I know. I can tell when people shudder."

"Wow." Caim dropped down on my other side. "You got Valac to smile. Can't say I see that every day."

"Maybe that's because you're not funny." I grinned.

Caim barked out a laugh and threw an arm around my shoulders. "I'm glad you're here, Mia. We might not remember you, but I think all of us felt like there was something missing in our lives. You fit into that hole perfectly."

Warmth flooded through me, loosening the tension in my shoulders. I jabbed my elbow into his side and rolled my eyes. "Don't get mushy on me now."

"Yes," Az said with ice in his voice as he stepped in front of us. He swirled his drink. Whiskey on ice. "Stop flirting with her, Caim."

I pressed my lips together. It was like nothing at all had changed. Valac was still very much Valac with his creepy mind-reading thing. Caim still joked around like he always did, and Az hated the idea that we might flirt. It almost felt like I was meant to be right here, surrounded by the Princes of Hell and my closest friends.

No matter what Lucifer had done to rip us apart, I always kept finding my way back to them.

He was going to lose his shit when he realized they'd gotten their memories back.

"Ten minutes." Serena hopped up from the floor and paced the length of the room. The coffee table was full of mugs, all containing droplets of our blood. The room fell silent as the moments ticked by. Gathered in a circle around the coffee table, we held our collective breath.

Midnight tolled, and my heart clanged like a cymbal of dread. Every eye in the room turned my way. I'd go first. With sweaty palms, I collected my mug from the table and held it over the candle's flame.

"Am I supposed to say something?" I whispered.

"Just think of lost memories," Stolas murmured from across the table. "Focus on what it is you need to relearn."

Okay. I could do that. I wanted to know about my past life as a fallen angel. There was so much I'd forgotten, things that might help us fight against Lucifer when the time came. Details about my time spent in Hell. Knowledge of his secrets. Anything at all that could give us an edge.

With a deep breath, I tipped my mug sideways and watched my blood drop onto the flame.

The world vanished. Everything went black.

A crown squatted on my head, heavy and binding. I gazed across the frozen landscape and breathed in the ice. The frost soothed my skin, and the chill filled my lungs with hope and life. The total opposite of those bastard flames in Hell.

"Archangel Mia." One of the fallen bowed before me, knees against the ice. She'd return from the mortal realm to beg forgiveness. Once the fallen left, they rarely came back. The Creator did not want Heaven corrupted by them.

"State your case," I said in a harsh voice. I didn't enjoy this part of my archangel status, but we all had to take our turn ruling the lesser angels and the fallen. It was our duty.

"The Creator is making a mistake," she implored.

I stiffened. "Excuse me?"

"He needs to give up this game." She looked up and met my eyes, her golden hair falling into her face. "Have you seen what it's like there? The humans aren't as terrible as you think. End the game and let them continue on living their—"

"I think I've heard enough," I snapped. "You've spent far too long in their presence, and they've corrupted you worse than I thought. You must remain fallen."

I snapped my fingers, and the world tunnelled around me.

*T*he Creator lounged on his throne. His skin was ice blue, and his brows were pure white. He wore nothing but a golden loin cloth cinched around his powerful waist and a sharp, thorny crown atop his head.

"I need you to do something for me, Mia," he drawled, his eyes half-lidded. Rumor had it, the Creator was never awake. He spent most of his time dozing on the throne while the world rotted away. Biding his time. Until he won the game.

Still, he was our king, and I was nothing if not loyal.

"Anything," I said.

"Lucifer is winning," he said with a grunt. "The tricky bastard."

I nodded. "He's very persuasive, I hear. The humans don't stand a chance against him and his Legions."

"I need you to find a way to stop him." He cracked open an eye. "By any means necessary."

I shifted on my feet. This was unexpected. Lucifer and the Creator had been playing the game of souls for centuries, and I'd never heard even a whisper of cheating. Whoever could tempt enough souls won. So far, they'd both played by the rules.

"I think I'm going to need you to be more specific," I said slowly. "Do you need me to search the ancient libraries for some kind of loophole or—"

"Leave Heaven, find a way to get close to him, and trick him into trusting you." The Creator chuckled. "Should be easy. He's dumb enough to fall for it."

"Leave Heaven," I repeated, my eyes drifting toward the archway that looked out on the Plains of Ice. Mile after mile of snow and frost. A land frozen for eternity.

And he wanted me to leave it all behind. I'd have to become one of the fallen.

His brow arched. "Is that a problem?"

"I don't want to leave. I don't want to become a fallen." I folded my arms and stepped back. "I'm not the right archangel for the job."

"Hmph." He snarled. "Very well. I'll make you a deal."

Interesting. The Creator rarely made deals. Most people just did what he told them to do, no questions asked.

"I'm listening," I said.

"Agree to this, and I'll gift you with immortality. Before you leave for Hell."

"I'm already immortal."

"Real immortality. You can never be stopped, not even if someone separates your heart from the rest of your body." He smiled when I let out a gasp. "That's right. I can make you indestructible. Even if someone scattered your body around the world, you'd come back. Your soul would find its way to another host."

"I'm in," I said quickly, before he could change his mind. My biggest fear had always been annihilation. Hundreds of years hadn't been enough. I wanted more. I wanted eternity.

The Creator's smile stretched wide. "Good. Prepare your things. You'll leave tonight."

Darkness consumed my mind.

J woke up panting with my hair plastered to my forehead. Peering through blurry eyes, I spotted the demons all crowded around me. Anger flashed in every eye, and tension pounded through the penthouse like a war drum.

"You're an archangel," Az growled, kneeling down beside me. "You've been lying to me this entire time."

I tried to make sense of his words, and the visions I'd just seen flickered in my mind like the reels of an old movie. They'd been nothing more than dreams...right? I couldn't be an *actual* archangel.

I didn't even know what an archangel was!

But I did know. Knowledge slid together in my mind like puzzle pieces. Those blurry memories were bursting with color now, and everything I'd done in my past life was bright, unyielding, and impossible to ignore.

I'd been an archangel. I'd left Heaven to take down Lucifer. And I had used Asmodeus to do it.

Shame flushed my neck and cheeks. There may have been feelings there, but they weren't what I'd thought they'd been. Taking down Lucifer had been far more important to me.

To her.

Never before had I been so certain that she and I were not the same, regardless of the soul we shared. I never would have done something like that. Not to the world. And certainly not to Az.

Shakily, I pushed up from the floor and gazed around at the Legion. I didn't know how to explain all of this to them. "Did you restore your memories?"

Az ground his teeth. "It didn't work."

"It got too late. The moment of midnight passed

before we could burn another drop of blood," Stolas filled in for him. "We were too distracted by..."

By me. It was then I noticed my hair. The brown was gone. In its place, the red had returned, blazing like the infernos of Hell. That spell had been powerful, alright. It had burned away the fae's glamor and revealed my forgotten memories.

"Well, then you've got to do it tomorrow night," I said. "When—"

"You need to get out of here now," Az growled as Phenex strode up behind him, slamming his fist against his open palm. "You've been lying to me. About things that are important. You've betrayed us all. I'll give you to the count of ten to get out of there."

Tears flooded my eyes. "Az. You can't be serious."

"I can't wait for him to let me have at you," Phenex said with a dark chuckle. "It's about goddamn time I get to take out one of the Creator's minions. Or are you Lucifer's? Doesn't matter. Either way, you're dead."

22

I ran through the Manhattan streets. My boots pounded the concrete, knocking my teeth together. Tears streamed down my face and blurred my vision, but I didn't care. My heart had been ripped in two. I could barely feel my lungs gasping for air.

My feet buckled beneath me, and I slammed against the ground. Arms trembling, I pushed up and wiped the grime from my face. This was by far the most horrible moment of my life, and I knew it would only get worse from here. Asmodeus hated me. With every fiber of his being.

Even if he got his memories back, I didn't know if that would change. I was his enemy. In my past life, I'd been just as wicked and as cruel as Lucifer said I was.

A taxi blasted by, its tires spinning through a puddle. Water sprayed across my face and stung my eyes. Wrinkling my nose, I scrabbled away from the edge of the sidewalk and pressed my back against the brick wall of the apartment building behind me. I hugged my knees to my chest and pulled the humid Manhattan air into my lungs.

This was pretty tragic, and I needed to take a moment to get a grip.

Let's think about this logically, Mia.

Right. So, the current situation sucked ass. The Legion, Serena, Priyanka, and Az had been right beside me when the archangel memories had rushed into my mind. And the spell had somehow revealed my origin to them, too. My glamors were also gone. That could pose a problem. I doubted I smelled like a werewolf now.

The biggest problem, of course, was that Asmodeus no longer believed anything I'd told him. That probably included the threat of Lucifer wanting him dead within a few days. All the progress I'd made in that direction had vanished like mist on a clear summer's day.

The others might still use the memory spell on themselves at midnight tomorrow. Maybe. If Az thought I was lying about everything, he could think I was lying about his lost memories, too. He might not do the spell without some prompting.

I needed someone to give him some prompting.

But who? It definitely couldn't be me.

I glanced up when a few New Yorkers scurried past, barely giving me a second glance. No doubt I looked deranged. I was squatting on a Hell's Kitchen sidewalk, soaked to my skin. My eyes were red and my hands were shaking. But I probably wasn't the weirdest thing they'd seen all day.

Anyway, back to the problem.

Who could help? Valac? Probably not.

It needed to be someone who hadn't been there tonight. Someone outside all of this, who didn't have an emotional investment. Someone on my side who wouldn't immediately turn me over to Az.

Someone like...Suriel and Gabriel.

Shakily, I pushed up from the ground, wondering if I well and truly had lost my mind. I couldn't go to the fallen angels. Could I? Who was to say they'd be happy to see me? It wasn't like we were friends.

But they knew me. We'd worked together. And they were one-hundred percent against Lucifer. They might have an idea on how to fix this. Something I hadn't thought of. And I doubted Lucifer would have thought to erase their memories of me. He might not even know we'd met.

Going to the angels wasn't my favorite idea, but it was the only one I had.

Now, I just had to find out where they lived.

The Legion probably knew, but it wasn't like I could ask them. Maybe they kept a record of addresses somewhere. A database of supernaturals who called the city home. It seemed like the kind of thing they'd do.

Time to break into *Infernal*.

🐚

*W*hen I strode into the Legion's meeting room, my eyes landed on the filing cabinets lined up along the back wall. I knew what those held. Records for the club's business activities, sure. But they *also* held records for the Legion's underground investigations.

I crossed the room and pulled open the top drawer. Flipping through the pages, I found contracts and bill payments for electricity, internet, and water. Not important.

Moving to the next drawer, I found employee contracts.

I let out a frustrated breath, but I wouldn't give up that easily. As the hour ticked by, I went through each and every folder until I arrived at the bottom drawer.

Inside, I struck gold. The folders were full of dossiers on supernaturals all throughout the city, including none other than Suriel and Gabriel. The pages listed detailed accounts of their activities over the past few months. And there it was. An address in Tribeca.

Bingo.

❧

*G*abe and Suriel lived on a pristine, tree-lined street with brownstone walkups and artsy wrought-iron street lamps. I stood at the base of their apartment building's front steps, wringing my hands.

Half of me was afraid they'd forgotten me, too. Half was afraid they hadn't. We hadn't exactly become friends back when we'd been thrown together, even though we'd ended up fighting on the same side. I'd pretty much told them they could go fuck themselves.

But I didn't know where else to go.

Filling my lungs with the humid, late-summer air, I strode up the steps and rang the bell. Static crackled a moment later, but no voice called out through the intercom. Frowning, I shoved my thumb against the bell again.

The door swung open. Suriel stood just inside the

entryway in a pair of dark sweatpants. His golden hair gleamed under the light of the street lamps, and his massive biceps looked like they'd been carved from stone.

His brows arched. "Is there something I can do for you?"

My heart plummeted to my feet. Shaking my head, I took a step back. This couldn't be happening. Not them, too. Lucifer had erased me from the memory of *everyone.* Mia McNally didn't exist anymore.

Once, I would have welcomed that. For so long, I'd tried to hide who I was. I'd wanted to vanish into the crowd and become someone else entirely.

Now that I had it, I didn't want it anymore. I wanted to be *me.* The good and the bad.

Suriel frowned. "Um, Earth to Mia? You going to answer me?"

I sucked in a sharp breath and flicked up my eyes to meet his. "You know who I am?"

His frown deepened. "Of course I do. What's going on, Mia? I was shocked enough to see you standing on my doorstep, and now you're acting very, very odd."

I wet my lips, shuddering. It was all I could do not to lurch toward him and bear hug his breath away. Someone remembered me. Someone supernatural.

"I just returned from Hell a few days ago, and no one remembers me but you," I blurted out.

Suriel stiffened. He cast his gaze around the street, nodded solemnly, and then opened the door wider. "In you come."

*S*uriel's house was nothing like I'd expected. Unlike the demons, the angels had gone to a lot of trouble to give their space a cozy, homey feel. The plush living space held three sofas covered in mounds of pillows. They formed three corners of a square that faced a television mounted on the wall. The hardwood floors were hidden beneath antique rugs swirling with red and gold patterns. Trinkets squatted on painted shelves, and framed photos hung along the walls. It looked like the home of a family, not two supernatural warriors.

Suriel returned with a cup of coffee and Gabe. The second of the two fallen angels didn't say a word as his gaze swept across me. He merely pushed his spiky black hair out of his eyes, settled on the sofa across from mine, and folded his hands in his lap.

Suriel handed me the coffee and remained standing. I didn't have the heart to tell him I hated the drink. He'd welcomed me into his home in the middle of the night, and *he remembered me*.

"When did you return from Hell?" Suriel asked, getting straight to business.

"A few days ago." I blew on the drink and wrapped my hands around the hot mug. "Things have been a bit of a whirlwind ever since. In the worst way possible."

"It must be bad. For you to come to us." Gabe leaned back and crossed an ankle over his knee. "I know we helped you that one time, but..."

"Let me guess. You're still not a fan of the Legion."

"We appreciate what they're trying to do," Suriel said. "And because of that, we won't interfere in their business. But no, I doubt we'll ever be friends with the

Princes of Hell. Not while the game of souls drives this world closer and closer to death and destruction."

"Well, I'm glad you brought that up. Because boy, do I have a story you're going to want to hear." Squaring my shoulders, I pulled a deep breath into my lungs and plowed forward, telling them everything. And I do mean everything. Now was not the time to hold anything back. It all came out. My archangel past. The memory loss. My deal to rip out Az's heart. It took me almost an hour to explain it all, and when I finally spoke the final words of the story, I felt drained.

Like all the blood had been sucked out of my veins.

"Lucifer made you a deal," Suriel repeated. "To rip out Az's heart."

"Yeah, afraid so."

"And you actually signed it?" Gabe's mouth had dropped open half an hour ago, and he still sat there like that. Totally gobsmacked. I couldn't blame him.

"I didn't have another choice," I whispered. "It's not like I would actually do it."

"Of course you wouldn't." Suriel began to pace. "He's clever, I'll give him that."

"Wait." I lifted my eyes to watch him stroll from one end of the room to the other. "What do you mean?"

He suddenly stopped. "You're not going to like what I have to say."

"It can't be that bad compared to everything else."

"Oh, yes it can," Gabe said quietly. "I know what Suriel is thinking, and I agree with him. You've been tricked."

A finger of ice slipped down my spine. Dread coiled around my heart, like a snake ready to strike. "Explain."

"Maybe you should drink your coffee," Suriel gently suggested.

"I don't think caffeine is a good idea right now. I already feel like my heart is going to bang its way out of my chest."

Suriel and Gabe exchanged a weighted glance. I didn't like this. The look on their faces chilled me to the bone. There was something they didn't want to tell me, and I had a horrible feeling it was going to shatter me. And I'd already broken into too many pieces tonight.

"I don't think Lucifer ever intended for you to rip out Az's heart," Suriel finally said. "He knows you wouldn't do it. You've fallen in love with him."

My stomach twisted. I wrapped my hands around the edge of the couch and squeezed tight. "Yeah, but he had me sign a contract. He thought that would get me to do it."

"No." Gabe shook his head, sighing. "He knew you'd only sign it as a way to get out of Hell. So that you could go back to Asmodeus. The memory loss is just him being a dick. A way to twist the knife in deeper. But he never thought you'd go through with it. He never thought you'd actually rip out Az's heart."

"I don't understand," I said, my heart thumping. "If that's really what he thinks, then what was the point of the deal? Just to torment me? Is that what this is about?"

"What were the terms of the deal, Mia?" Suriel murmured.

"I..." I frowned. "My soul, of course. Isn't that what it always is?"

Gabe gave me a solemn nod. "That's what a demon deal always is."

"But I don't understand. He wants my soul?"

"Do you know what an immortal archangel's soul is worth? One that will always be reincarnated?" Suriel asked, steepling his fingers beneath his chin. "It's far more than a human's soul."

My stomach dropped. Oh my god. My soul. How had I not seen it before now? He didn't care about Az. It was me all along.

Tricky bastard.

"I'm not sure I want to know," I finally said around the lump of ice in my throat.

"It's enough. More than enough. Lucifer is so far ahead in the game that he wouldn't need more than that," Suriel said, his eyes darkening. "If he gets your soul, everything is over. Hell wins."

23

The city was quiet up here on the roof. A light wind rustled my hair, bringing with it the stench of garbage and taxi fumes. After our conversation, I'd needed some air. It was a lot to process. Not only had Lucifer tricked me, but he'd done a damn good job of it.

He'd pretty much trapped me in an impossible situation. If I followed through on the terms of the deal, I'd lose Az. But if I didn't, not only would he continue the game but he would *win* it. Immediately. Funny how he hadn't mentioned that when he'd given me the offer.

He'd been lying through his teeth the entire time. All to back me into a corner. I wondered what that meant for the prophecy, the one that said Az and I would end the world. That had probably been a lie, too.

Suriel dropped down beside me, crouching on the red-brick ledge. His wings flared behind him, silver against the shadows of the night. "You alright?"

"Not really, no." I sighed and propped my elbows on

the ledge, leaning over as far as I could without falling. This situation sucked. To put it mildly.

"I think you know what I'm going to say," he said gently. "And I'd prefer if you listen instead of flying off the handle."

I rolled my eyes. "Thanks for assuming I'll fly off the handle."

"You might have to give Lucifer what you promised him."

"No." I pushed away from the ledge and stalked across the rooftop. "Absolutely not."

Suriel followed. "And you'd let the world end just like that? Flames and hellbeasts for everyone?"

My hands fisted as I whirled toward him. "It's not ideal, but it's probably not the worst option. I've been to Hell. It really wasn't that bad."

He arched a brow. "What part of Hell?"

"The capital or whatever. Where Lucifer lives."

"Allyria?" he asked.

"Yeah." I started pacing the roof again. "It was almost like a normal old city. One from like *Game of Thrones* or something, but it wasn't so bad. A few flames here and there. An intense heat. But it wasn't anything like I'd expected. No torture. No monsters. Nothing like that."

"Lucifer took you to the only part of Hell where none of that is allowed," Suriel said softly. "The city is his haven. His home. Besides, you were with him. No one would dare go near you with him by your side. Not unless he called upon them."

Frowning, I thought back to my time there. In the deserts, he'd never left my side. In the city, I'd spent most of my time locked up in that room.

"So, you're telling me human souls aren't safe in Allyria?"

"Mia, human souls aren't allowed in that city. It's *his* home. And the home of his most loyal demons. All the terrible parts of Hell are elsewhere. Lucifer doesn't like to shit where he eats."

"He lied to me," I whispered. "About everything."

"Very much so." He paused. "He's the King of Hell. What did you expect?"

I slumped to the ground and dropped my head into my hands. I couldn't believe how gullible I'd been. "He was so convincing...he made it out like he was trying to stop the world from freezing over. Said he wanted to save everyone..."

"Well, that part was the truth. Lucifer doesn't want the world to freeze over," he said. "But it's not because he cares about humanity. He just wants Hell to win."

The thunder of wings broke through our conversation. I tipped back my head to gaze up at the sky. Az and his Legion stormed toward us on a whirlwind of black feather wings. Suriel jumped in front of me, blocking my body with his.

Az landed in a crouch, shadows whorling around his powerful body. The rest of the Legion stayed in the sky, circling the building like a swarm of angry bees. My heart hammered my ribs. Maybe this was a good thing. Maybe he'd tracked me down to apologize...

Ha!

I swallowed hard at the look on his face. Nope. This definitely wasn't a friendly conversation.

"Valac told me about your deal." Az's commanding voice boomed like thunder. "With Lucifer."

My eyes flicked toward the Legion. There were only

four of them, and Valac wasn't there. That must have been a fun conversation. It hurt that Valac had told Az about the deal, but at the same time, I couldn't blame him.

"It's not what you think," I said, turning back to him. "I only signed it so I could get out of Hell."

He growled. "Do you really expect me to believe that after all the other lies you told me? Let me guess. That sob story about your trial wasn't true either. Because I couldn't find a record of it anywhere."

My mouth dropped open. "What?"

Had Lucifer erased that from the world, too?

"That's right." He stalked toward me. "I know everything, Mia. You came here to rip out my heart and thought seducing me was the best way to pull it off. Well, now I know the truth. You've been my enemy all along."

"Mia," Suriel warned as he held his arms out on either side of his body. "Stay back."

Az glanced at Suriel, his eyes flashing with rage. "I'm glad, at least, that you came here. All of my enemies together."

"I'm not your enemy either, Asmodeus," Suriel said in a quiet, calm voice I didn't know how he could manage. "I know you don't remember Mia, but surely you haven't forgotten when we teamed up to take down the Covenant Ball a couple of months ago."

Gabe landed just behind me. He must have heard the commotion. "We're all on the same side, Asmodeus. And you need to calm down. No one here is your enemy."

"Calm down?" Az laughed. "I can't believe you're

spouting the same shit that she is. It's over. For all of you. Five against three."

All the blood drained from my face. I'd never seen him look so angry. Like he wanted to rip all the limbs off my body and burn them to the bone. He probably did. That was why the Legion had come here. They planned to take care of their foes once and for all.

And to them, I was the ultimate enemy.

"Don't hurt him," I whispered to Suriel's back. "He doesn't understand what's going on. None of them do."

"Mia." Gabe stepped up behind me, sandwiching me between him and Suriel's back. A double shield of fallen angels. "Now might be the time to do what's necessary to stop Lucifer from winning the game."

My entire body burned with a terrible heat, far worse than the flames of Hell. "I won't do it. I can't. I know that makes me weak. I know it makes me selfish. But I can't. No matter what it means, I can't."

Gabe sighed against me, but he didn't push any harder, even though I thought he might. Neither one of the fallen angels had any loyalty toward Az. To them, he was just another Prince of Hell. An easy sacrifice for a better world. Lucky for me, they weren't the ones who got the choice.

"Alright then," he murmured. "If that's your decision, then we'll have to find another way."

His strong arms wrapped around my body, and he shot up into the clouds. Suriel darted to the left and then to the right, moving so fast he was nothing more than a blur. The Legion shouted and charged, but we'd caught them off guard. They hadn't expected us to flee.

We shot through the clouds. My cheeks rattled from the force of the wind. Nausea rose up in my throat, threatening to spill down the front of my shirt. Az had never flown this fast with me, and now I understood why. I felt like I was being whipped up in a blender, like I didn't know up from down and left from right.

"They're still behind us," Suriel shouted as he shot up beside us. "We need to go faster."

My stomach flipped.

"Faster?" I eked out.

Gabe's hands slipped along my sweat-soaked arms, and a scream lodged in my throat. If I fell...

"Hold on tight," he murmured into my ear. "We need to lose them."

"Blergh," was all I could manage. Still, I gripped onto his neck and dug my fingernails into his skin. Facing an angry Legion would almost be preferable right now. Gabe zoomed forward faster until the world far below my dangling feet was nothing more than a rolling blur.

"Where are we going?" I asked, squeezing my eyes shut to block out the ground.

"We need to mask your scent. We're going to the fae."

24

"Az isn't stupid. He knows I'll try to get another glamor." I stood on the Brooklyn Bridge, folded over the top of the railing and staring down at the river. My whole body felt like jelly. As soon as my feet had touched the ground, my adrenaline had *whooshed* right out of my system, leaving me broken and dazed.

I *never* wanted to do that again.

Collapsed against the railing, I breathed in the scent of fish and river water. The moon reflected off the surface, and the building lights flickered in the inky black. It was way too much movement. Another burst of nausea choked my throat.

I closed my eyes, thankful it was the middle of the night. There were still a few passersby, but the bridge wasn't packed like it was in broad daylight. Fewer witnesses.

"You done throwing up yet?" Suriel asked from where he perched beside me.

I moaned, wishing the world could swallow me

whole. "That was the worst thing I've ever experienced in my life. Who taught you how to fly like that?"

He grunted. "I taught myself to fly, just like everything else. Gabe and I left Heaven not long after we were born."

Blearily, I pulled back to gaze up at him. "You were born?"

"Of course we were. What did you think? That we just poofed into existence?"

"I don't know." I sighed, closing my eyes again. "Past Mia's memories flooded my brain, and there are way too many for me to make sense of it all."

"It will take you time to process things. You basically have two people inside your head."

"When you say it like that, you make me sound crazy."

"She's coming." Gabe dropped down beside us and folded his wings into his back. The angels were far more obvious about their supernatural status than the demons were. Everyone in Az's Legion seemed intent on secrecy. The only time Az had ever opened his wings in front of humans, we'd been on the run from the King of Hell.

"I thought there was a rule," I said, pushing away from the railing. "We're not supposed to let humans know about us."

Us. Like I was one of them. But even with an archangel soul, this body was very much human.

Gabe waved his hand dismissively. "There's hardly anyone on the bridge, and I don't feel like pussyfooting around it. We have an angry Legion tracking you down. The sooner we get this over with, the better."

Sadness ballooned around my heart. It had hurt, seeing Az look at me like that. Even when he hadn't remembered me, there'd still been some softness there. Wary softness, but still. He'd been willing to give me a chance. He certainly hadn't shot daggers at me with his eyes.

If the fallen angels weren't so good at flying, I hated to imagine what he might have done.

"You okay?" Suriel bent down, concern furrowing the lines on his face. "I know you were hoping to smooth things over, and instead..."

Instead, Az wanted to kill me.

"No, I'm not okay." I shrugged. "But I can't focus on that right now."

If I did, it might bring me to my knees.

Just like Lucifer wanted.

"The fae will demand a favor in return for your scent glamor," Gabe said. "Just to warn you, she might call upon it at any time, and it will likely be something you don't want to do."

"Yeah, I know how it works." I sighed. "I already owe one of them a favor."

In the distance, a curvy figure with curly purple hair strode down the middle of the bridge. Her hips swayed to an invisible beat, and a sly smile whispered across her full, painted lips. Frowning, I shot a sharp glance at Suriel.

"That's River. The same fae I've met before. She's friendly with Az." I took two hurried steps back. I wasn't ready to face him again. Not yet. If he came at us with his full force, the fallen angels might decide to fight him this time.

They wouldn't hold back if he threatened their lives.

"Don't worry. She knows how to be discreet." Gabe

lifted his hand when she sashayed in front of us. "Hello, love. Nice to see you again."

"Gabe. Suriel. You're looking well, if a little ruffled." River gave me a once-over, laughed, and then propped her hand on her hip. "I'd say I'm surprised to see you again, but I'm not. What's happened now? I see you got rid of your other glamors. Let me guess. You want them back."

"Not those specifically," I said slowly. "I need an entirely different scent. One that will fully mask who I am."

Her brows shot up. "You're on the run again. Who's looking for you this time?"

"I can't tell you that," I said tensely.

"Ha." She shook her head. "It's our dear Asmodeus then. What's it about this time?"

I glanced up at Gabe, who merely shrugged. "The fae have loyalty to no one but themselves. If you decide to tell her, the worst she'll do is tell everyone inside her court."

"I mean, that's probably not ideal," I said. "We're doing this so Az and the Legion can't track me down. If half of the supernatural community know about my new scent, I might as well just keep the one I have."

"This is serious, isn't it? Interesting." River took a step closer and sniffed. "I'm not like Asmodeus. I can't sniff out your emotions, but I *can* tell that you've been burning your own blood. Tell me what's happened. I can't help you if you don't explain what's going on."

"It's a very long story," I whispered.

Suriel rolled his eyes. "Basically, Lucifer wants Mia's soul. To keep it, she has to rip out Az's heart. She obviously will never do that, but Az doesn't know. He can't remember their bond. He thinks she plans on doing it. So, he's tracking her."

I glared at him. "I really think we should have kept that to ourselves."

"Why does Lucifer want a fallen angel's soul?" River asked, focusing on what I did not think was our biggest problem right now. It was Az, his heart, and the hunt.

"She's an archangel," Gabe murmured. "An immortal one to boot."

"Oh." River's eyes flew wide. "Well, fuck."

"So, can you help me?" I asked. "I just need a glamor to hide my scent, and then I swear I'll never come to you for anything ever again."

"Yeah," she muttered. "You'll never come to me because I won't be here anymore. We'll all be in Hell."

"Bit dramatic," I muttered.

"But it's the truth." She ran her fingers through her purple hair and bit her bottom lip. "Lucifer will win if he gets your soul."

"Yeah, I know."

"You have to do something," she insisted, throwing up her hands. "This is Hell we're talking about, Mia. We'll all be doomed to a life of eternal torment."

"I've tried doing something." My voice cracked, and tears filled my eyes. "I've been trying. Okay? Trust me. I don't want this to happen any more than you do, but Lucifer knew how to back me into an impossible corner. He knows I won't kill Az. And don't you dare fucking tell me I should do it. Because I won't. I'll do *anything*, but I won't do that."

"Alright, okay." She held up her hands, and I couldn't help but notice they were shaking. "Let's just...get this over with, okay? The longer we stand here

199

arguing, the more likely it is that Az will find you here. And I don't think that will be good for any of us."

Letting out a long sigh, I nodded. "Good. The glamor then. Can you just give me one that's human?"

"You'll owe me a favor," she said.

"I know."

With a smile, she pressed a hand to my shoulder. Sparks lit up along my skin, burning me up from the inside out. I gritted my teeth as the pain flared hot, and then it slowly faded to nothing but a dull ache.

My fallen angel scent was gone. Thank god.

"This is the second favor you owe me," she added. "Which means I'm calling on one of them right now."

Dread curled around my heart. "No. Uh uh. I know what you're going to say, and you can't ask me to do that. It's not fair."

"You need to end this, Mia," she warned. "I won't accept anything else."

I blew out a frustrated breath. "At least give me a chance to find another way. There's still time for me to make this right."

"No." She pressed her lips together. "The only way this works is if you give Lucifer exactly what he wants."

"What he wants is my soul," I argued. "And we've all agreed I can't give that to him."

Her eyes softened. "I meant Az's heart, and you know it."

"Yeah," I said slowly. "He wants a heart."

Wait a minute...

"You've got a funny look on your face," Gabe said with a chuckle. "You alright in there?"

"A heart," I repeated, eyes widening.

"I think we broke her," Suriel sighed. "She's an

archangel in a human body. Does she need to eat or something?"

"Probably sleep," Gabe said. "I think they malfunction if they don't get eight hours."

"I'm supposed to deliver Az's heart to Lucifer," I said in a small voice. "The thing is...how will he know it's *Az's* heart?"

"Oh." River's eyes went as wide as dinner plates. "I see where you're going with this. You want to use a decoy."

"Yeah," I said as a slow smile spread across my face. Lucifer was a tricky bastard. Best way to beat one of those? Become trickier than he could ever imagine. "Where do we get ahold of a heart? A morgue or something?"

"Nah," Suriel said with a frown. "It has to be a demon heart. They're bigger than human hearts."

"What about a fallen angel's?" I asked dryly.

"That wouldn't work either," Gabe growled. "But nice try."

I grinned. "Just needed to check."

"He's right though." River sighed. "You need a demon heart. Otherwise, it won't work."

"So, we just need to find a demon, destroy him, and rip out his heart." I winced. "One of the bad demons, obviously. There are some in Manhattan, right?"

"It's not that easy to destroy a demon," Suriel said. "If it was, there would be far more missing demons like Morax in the world."

My head slowly swivelled to the side. I stared at Suriel, wondering if I could have possibly heard him right. Morax. A strange sensation rushed along the back of my neck, prickling up as a thousand goosebumps.

"Morax," I breathed.

River cocked her head. "You look like you've just seen a ghost."

"Morax's heart," I said a little more excitedly. This was by far the best idea I'd ever had in my life. "Eisheth knows where it is. If I can manage to wrangle that information out of her, I can find Morax's heart and take it to Lucifer. He'll have no idea where it really came from, and we won't have to destroy anyone in order to pull it off."

"Not bad, Mia." Suriel let out a low whistle. "The only problem is, Eisheth would go straight to Lucifer and tell him everything."

I waved my hand dismissively. "We'll throw her in a dungeon or something."

"Well, this is escalating quickly. What about Az? Lucifer will probably check to make sure he's gone from the world."

"It's the dungeon for him, too. At least until Lucifer ends the game." I grinned. "This gives Lucifer exactly what he wants, I keep my soul, and Az doesn't die. It's perfect. It solves everything."

"The only problem is," Gabe cut in. "Eisheth doesn't know where Morax's heart is. Her memories of where she hid him are gone."

"Don't worry. I know a way to get around that. With midnight, a candle, and blood."

25

"So, you're going to trap Asmodeus and Eisheth, find Morax's heart, *and* trick Lucifer...all in one night?" Gabe frowned. "That's quite the plan."

Exactly." I nodded my head in satisfaction. "Easy peasy."

I knew it would not be easy peasy, but I was riding on the high of my brilliant idea. Game. Set. Match. *Take that, Lucifer!* He'd never know what hit him.

Damn, he was going to lose his mind when he realized I'd tricked him, but it would be too late for him to course correct at that point. He'd have forfeited the game before he knew the heart belonged to someone else. By then, it would all be over.

And the world would continue. No ice or flames destroying everything. No torture. No hellbeasts. Perfect.

"Mia," Suriel said gently. "Now, I mean this with all the respect I can muster, but...you're just a mortal girl. Why do you think we fled from the Legion? You don't really stand a chance against them. You don't have the strength to trap Asmodeus, especially if he puts up a fight."

"You're right," I said. "*I* don't."

"Oh no," Gabe muttered. "I see where this is going now."

"You, on the other hand, have a decent chance. If you team up together and catch him off guard, I bet you can do it." I grinned when they both threw up their hands. "Are you saying you're too scared to face the Big, Bad Asmodeus?"

"I think I'd prefer not to have my wings ripped off my back, thanks," Suriel said. "Mia, he's stronger than you think."

"You just have to knock him out long enough for you to get him into a dungeon cell." I shrugged. "Use some valium or something. Sneak up on him from behind with a tranquilizer gun. Do whatever you need to do."

"I'm not a big fan of this plan," Gabe said, rustling his spiky hair. "Couldn't we try something simpler?"

"Like what?" I asked. "You want me to rip out his heart? Then, I will use your exact argument against you. I'm just a human girl. I don't have the strength. He's stronger than you—"

"Alright, alright." Gabe held up a hand. "I get it."

"We'll do it," Suriel said firmly. "On one condition. You have to find that heart first. If you don't, we're not touching Asmodeus."

"Sounds like a deal to me." I turned to River. "And you'll keep this quiet?"

She shrugged. "Hell, you're fulfilling your end of the bargain, and I won't do anything to ruin that. Go get that fucking heart and give it to the King of Hell."

❀

I knocked on the door. The fallen angels stood on either side of me. It was a risk coming here, but there had to be a reason Valac hadn't joined the Legion when they'd decided to chase me down.

He'd told Az about the deal, but that didn't mean he wanted to see me dead. At least I hoped not.

The door cracked open, and pure white eyes stared out at me. Valac let out a huff of irritation and started to slam the door in my face. I kicked out my boot to block him.

"I need you to hear me out," I said. "It's not what it looks like."

"I don't even know what it looks like, Mia. All I know is you kept the truth from all of us. Including me."

"I didn't know about the archangel thing, okay?" I argued. "Not until everyone else did. Lucifer messed with my memories, too."

He hesitated, and I could see that I'd gotten to him.

"At least let me try to explain," I tried.

"If Az knew you were here, he'd lose his goddamn mind. And why do you have two fallen angels with you?" He flicked his eyes back and forth from face to face. "I don't like it. They can't come in here."

"Fine with me," Gabe grunted.

I nodded at Gabe and Suriel before pushing into the apartment. Valac stood in the center of his floor, clad in black sweatpants and a grey tee. He looked so normal like this, except for the bleached white hair and the piercing, all-knowing gaze. And the intense power. And the muscles that were bigger than my head. Okay, so he didn't look at all normal.

"Go on then." He folded his arms. "Tell me what you came here to say."

"Lucifer tricked me," I said plaintively. "He wants my soul. My immortal archangel soul that apparently is worth a hell of a lot in that damn game. And if I don't deliver him a demon heart, he's going to get it. Hell wins."

He pursed his lips. "I thought as much."

"You did?"

"I've been thinking about it all night. Your deal. Your soul. Your past life as an archangel. It didn't make sense that he'd want Az's heart. What would that do for him?"

"He told me Az and I would end the world together, and that's why he wanted me to kill him. To stop that from ever happening." I let out a rattling breath. "Pretty sure that was just one of his many lies."

"Exactly." Valac nodded. "So, I figured, if he doesn't want Az dead, what's he really after? It became pretty clear tonight when your archangel memories came flooding back."

"So, if you figured it out, why did Az come after me like that?" I winced at the memory. "I've never seen him that angry."

He shook his head and sighed. "As soon as I tried to explain things to him, he jumped to conclusions. I mentioned the deal, and that was it. He was gone before I got to the part about your soul. There was nothing I could do to stop him."

"It's not your fault." I paced the room, thinking.

"You didn't come here just to clear the air." Valac's gaze pierced me. "I can read you better now that I know what your soul is. There's something you want from me."

A chill swept down my spine. "You're way too good at that, Valac. If I didn't love you, I'd find you creepy as hell."

"Love." His lips tilted up in the corners. "You love the Legion?"

"Of course I do." I stopped and placed my hands on his shoulders so that I could, for once, look deeply into his eyes. "You guys have become my family. For better or worse. I swear to you that I would never do a single one of you harm."

"Even if it meant the end of the world," he murmured.

I closed my eyes. "Goddamn it. Even if it meant the end of the world."

A moment passed in silence. The only sound was the heavy thump of my heart. Valac reached up and squeezed my hand. He rarely showed emotion, but I swore I could feel it pouring off of him now.

"What do you need me to do?" he asked quietly.

Resolve solidified in my gut. We were going to do this. "I need to know where Eisheth lives."

Shock flickered across his face. He hadn't been expecting that. "Eisheth? Why?"

"I'm going to restore her memories." A beat passed. "Of where she hid Morax's heart."

Valac drew back, blinking rapidly. "Morax's heart."

"I know it's not ideal, using Morax's heart to trick Lucifer, but I won't let him hold on to it. He just needs to see it and think Az is dead." I stumbled over my words a bit, but I kept going. I knew this was the right call, even if it might upset him. Morax had been one of the Legion. A brother to them all. "And then we can find the rest of him. Bring him back."

Valac dragged a hand down his face and shuddered violently. I pressed my fingers to my lips, wondering if I'd made the wrong call. I hadn't expected him to react like this. Upset? Maybe. Uneasy? Sure. But he seemed well and truly rocked to the core.

"Valac?" I whispered.

"Eisheth would never reveal Morax's location, even if she could remember it. She doesn't want us to know."

"We'll find a way," I insisted. "Besides, can you think of a better plan?"

He jammed his fingers into his hair and paced the length of the room, muttering to himself. His eyes were wild. His body thrummed with pent-up energy. I'd never seen him like this before, like he was a wild animal. Caged. Normally, Valac was calm, composed, and quiet. He huddled in the corner, watching everything with piercing eyes.

Right now, he was acting like he might explode.

"I've got to be honest, Valac. You're freaking me out a bit."

Finally, he stopped in the middle of the floor. "You have no idea what you've just said."

"You're right." My hands hung heavily by my sides. "I can never really understand what you've been through and how you feel about Morax. I know you don't want Lucifer to get near his heart, but...just think about what this would mean. It would solve everything."

He shuddered. "Eisheth doesn't know where Morax's heart is."

I blinked. "What?"

"She knows where his body is. Or she did, before

Lucifer erased her memories." He ground his teeth together. "But she does not have his heart. We do."

I gaped at him. "*You* have it?"

"Az spent decades trying to track Morax down. He roamed the Earth for years. And he *did* find something. A part of him. His heart." Valac swallowed hard. "It's a secret we swore we'd never reveal. To anyone. If Eisheth or Lucifer ever found out we had ahold of it, they would find a way to take it from us. And it's all we have left of him."

"Oh." And here I was, asking Valac to give it up. I needed to sit down. "I see."

"Az keeps it in his penthouse. In a trunk underneath his bed."

"Ohhhh." I nodded. "That explains a lot."

The locks, the wards, the secrecy. I'd always known he was hiding something inside that room. I'd just never guessed it was this.

"The only way to get the trunk open is by punching in the right number combination. Nothing else would ever work, not even trying to detonate a bomb beside it. It's indestructible. The witches made sure of that."

I looked up, heart thumping. "Why are you telling me all this, Valac?"

He rubbed his hand against his jaw, still shuddering. "Because I think you have to do it. It's what Morax would want. He always dreamed of saving the world, even if it meant the ultimate sacrifice. If Lucifer gets his hands on that heart, we might never see it again."

"I won't let him keep it, Valac." My voice cracked from the sheer emotion charging through the room. "I won't even let him touch it."

"You might not have a choice, Mia," he whispered

back. "If he thinks it's Az's heart, he'll do his best to take it away from you. We'll never see Morax again."

Tears spilled onto my cheeks. "Oh, Valac."

He strode across the floor and grasped my hands in his. "I'm going to help you do this. You just have to promise me one thing."

"What's that?" I whispered as the tears splashed onto my lips.

"When all of this is over, you'll help me get that heart back. And then we'll find the rest of him."

I nodded. "It's a deal. We'll get Morax back, no matter how long it takes."

26

The problem with sneaking into an angry demon's penthouse apartment was three-fold.

1. He had wards to alert him of intruders, and I was definitely an intruder at this point.

2. He'd sulked on his sofa for the better part of the day, making it impossible to sneak inside undetected.

3. I was pretty sure he expected me to come back, so it wasn't out of the realm of possibility that he'd set a trap. What that trap would be remained to be seen. Az thought I was here to rip out his heart. He wouldn't let his guard down.

After some brainstorming, Valac found an excuse to drag Az away for a few hours. Someone had tried to break into *Infernal*, and the Legion needed to count the inventory and file a report with the cops. Clearly, no one had *actually* tried to break in. We'd just made it look that way after taking out the security cameras. It would keep him busy for a couple of hours at least.

As soon as he was gone, the four of us flew to the balcony. Well, three of us flew. Me, on the other hand, did my whole cling-on routine and prayed for a swift death if I fell. When we landed on the balcony, I tried to pretend like I wasn't bothered, but my racing heart gave me away. I really hated flying.

We all faced Az's penthouse.

The sliding glass doors were open. Almost welcoming.

Hendrix soared in behind me and landed on my shoulder. Poor thing probably had no idea what the hell was going on these days. I couldn't wait for things to get back to normal for him. *If* I could get things back to normal. And that was one big if.

"What do we do about the wards?" I asked. We didn't know any witches, so we didn't have a way of dismantling them. The second we stepped inside, silent alarms would alert Az of our arrival.

"We'll just have to be quick," Valac said. "We go in, grab the trunk, and then you three will fly away with it. I'll wait here instead of going with you. When he sees me, he'll realize it wasn't an actual break-in."

Would he, though?

"Except he'll be able to smell us" Gabe said with a frown. "The fallen angel scent is strong. It will linger here."

Valac lifted a bag, and glass clinked together. "I'll light some candles."

I arched a brow. "You brought a bag of candles?"

"He's going to think that's really weird, Valac," Suriel said.

"Possibly, but I've done stranger things. Listen, you three get the trunk." He patted my shoulder. "I'll take care of Asmodeus. I'm part of his Legion. The worst he will do is shout at me. You, on the other hand..."

I held up my hand and nodded. "No need to finish. I get the picture."

Az thought I intended him and his Legion harm, and he would do anything to protect his own. Right now, I was very much not his own.

"So, do you understand the plan?" Valac asked.

"Yeah." I turned toward the angels. "You ready?"

On the count of three, we all rushed inside the penthouse. The living room held the remnants of last night's seance. Candles and blood mugs littered the coffee table, and empty pizza boxes were scattered across the floor. Asmodeus really must have been shaken, not to clean up. That wasn't like him. He liked his place spic and span.

And it was all my fault.

A pang of remorse went through me, but I couldn't focus on that right now. We needed to get in and out before he returned.

Az's bedroom door was locked, as always. He'd had the busted wood replaced since the last time I'd broken inside. Unfortunately for him, he shouldn't have bothered. I hauled back my foot to slam it open, but Valac bustled past with a golden key in his hand.

"Stop. We don't want it to look like anyone actually broke in." He slid the key in the lock. "Stand back."

"Oh." I dropped my foot to the floor. Too bad. I would have enjoyed slamming my boot into something. Since we weren't going after Eisheth, a door was the next best thing. Better luck next time.

When the door swung wide, Suriel and Gabe bustled over to the bed. They hauled the trunk into their arms and raced back out onto the balcony. I just stood there watching them, feeling a little left out of the whole thing. I'd come here to help.

"Well, I guess they've got it, huh?" I said with a wry smile.

"Yes, and you better get going." Valac jerked his thumb toward the sliding doors. "Az will get back any minute, and you don't want him to catch you here."

"Alright." I took two steps toward the door and paused. "Are you sure you'll be okay?"

His luminous eyes lit up the dark apartment. "I'll be fine. But you won't be. That's why you have to go, Mia. *Now.*"

I nodded and backed out the door. "See you soon, Valac. And don't forget to restore your memories tonight."

With a deep breath, I raced out onto the balcony to join the angels. Each one gripped a handle of the trunk, and it swung wildly between them. Suriel's face blazed bright red as he grunted from the effort.

"This thing is heavier than I thought it would be," Gabe muttered.

I swallowed hard. "Yeah, it weighs like a million pounds. Are you going to be able to carry it?"

"Yeah, but." Suriel frowned. "It's going to be next to impossible to carry you, too."

All the blood drained out of my face. I jerked my chin over my shoulder to stare at the apartment door that led to the elevator. Maybe if I hurried, I could get out of the building before Az got back.

"I can go on my own," I said, turning back to them. "That trunk is the most important thing."

"Absolutely not," Gabe said firmly. "We're not leaving you behind. Climb on."

I shifted on my feet. This didn't seem like a good idea, but neither did the alternative. One way, I might tumble to my death if the angels couldn't hold on to me. The other, I might come face to face with a Prince of Hell who thought I'd betrayed him.

Could there be a third option?

"Maybe I could just hide?" I tried.

"Climb on," Suriel growled. "Stop stalling. We don't have much time."

Dammit, I was going to have to take the flight option. With a frustrated breath, I stepped in close to Gabe and wrapped my arms around his neck. We were off before I'd braced myself for what was to come.

The world dropped out from beneath me as the angels hurtled over the Manhattan rooftops. They jerked wildly, the trunk dragging them left and right. We suddenly dropped what felt like a mile. My heart leapt into my throat and stuck there. I was going to die.

"Hold on, Mia," Gabe shouted into my ear.

I clutched his neck tighter and ground my teeth as he released his grip on my waist. He groaned as he grabbed the handle with both hands, but it didn't help. We lurched toward the ground like a plane nosediving straight to total catastrophe.

"This isn't going to work," Suriel called out, getting control for a split second, just long enough to slow the descent.

A second later, we tumbled into the middle of the street. My knees slammed into the pavement, knocking my teeth together. It took me a moment to hear anything more than a loud ringing in my ears and the blood boiling through my veins.

Gabe knelt before me, gently took my arms, and

215

helped me to my feet. "I'm sorry. We can't carry both you and the trunk."

I blinked the spots out of my eyes. "You're fallen angels. Shouldn't you be stronger than this?"

"That trunk is supernaturally heavy, Mia." Suriel sighed and dragged a hand down his face. "Az no doubt made it this way so that it would be impossible to steal."

"Not impossible," I pointed out. "We *did* get it."

Thank god. We had Morax's heart. The plan was actually coming together. We just needed to get the trunk off this street and hidden somewhere safe until tonight.

"We're going to have to take the trunk and leave you here," Suriel said with a wince. "Then, we'll come back and get you. We won't be long."

"It's okay." I glanced around us. It was a quiet alley with dark buildings rising up on either side. No lights were on in the windows. Thankfully, no one had seen a thing. "I can start walking to wherever you're taking it."

"You should stay here," Gabe said. "This is hidden and out of the way. Keep out of sight. Az might be looking for you." He turned to Suriel. "We'll have to fly low ourselves. We can't risk him spotting us in the sky."

Suriel nodded. "He's likely returned to his penthouse by now. We don't know how long Valac will be able to distract him from the missing trunk."

A shiver raced down my spine. If Az realized what we'd taken, he'd be out for blood. My blood.

"Go," I said to them. "Just don't take too long, okay? Squatting in a dark alley for hours isn't really my idea of a good time."

The angels nodded, grasped the impossibly heavy trunk, and lumbered up into the sky, staying below the line of rooftops. I watched them hurtle away, my hands helpless beside me. If only I had wings, life would be so much easier.

I kicked a tin can and shoved my hands into my pockets. This plan had to work. It was the only one we had, and I didn't know what we'd do if it all went wrong. The taste of imminent victory was sweet on my tongue, but it would quickly turn sour if the wind blew wrong.

Wings pounded the air above my head. Thank god. The angels were back already. I tipped back my head to wave, but it was Asmodeus who hurtled toward the street. He landed in a crouch, snarling.

My heart rattled. He'd found me.

"Nice try." Az stalked toward me, squaring his shoulders. "Did you really think you could get away with stealing from me?"

Swallowing hard, I glanced around the empty alley. Nothing to use as a weapon. Nowhere to hide. Gabe and Suriel needed to get back here. Pronto. "Look at me. I don't have anything that belongs to you."

"I know you took my trunk, Mia." His gaze narrowed. "Tell me where it is, before I do something we'll both regret."

"Funny," I said. "Because from where I'm standing, I don't think you'd regret it one bit."

"Tell me where it is," he demanded, his voice booming all around us.

I took a slow step back. "The thing is, Az, I don't actually know."

A dangerous growl rumbled from his throat, and goosebumps popped up on every inch of my skin. His eyes flashed with rage, and shadows whipped through the empty street, spinning like tornados from Hell. "You have no idea what you've done. I will make you pay for this."

"How about you wait for midnight, restore your memories, and *then* we can have this conversation? You might find that you see things very differently."

At least, I hoped he would. It was starting to feel impossible that he would ever look at me the way he once had.

"You must be delusional to think I'd ever listen to a damn word you said."

"Maybe. But if everything was a lie, why would I keep up the charade now? You heard the truth about my soul last night."

"Because." He spat at the ground. "You plan to destroy my entire Legion. Why else would you have stolen Morax's heart?"

Alright. Clearly, I wasn't going to talk him down from his mountain of rage. He thought I'd stolen Morax's heart, which...I had, actually. But he wouldn't understand why, not so long as he refused to restore his memories.

I was his greatest enemy. More so than Lucifer right now. I'd stolen Morax. His brother. His home. All this time, he'd kept ahold of his heart, hoping to find a way back to him.

I'd seen the pain in his eyes when he'd spoken of Morax.

What I'd done was like a stab in the heart, twisted sideways for maximum damage. I wish he could understand, just because it would take the pain away. As it was, he was mad as hell.

I had to get out of here before he took that rage out on me.

I gave him maybe twenty seconds tops before he rushed me.

Shaking, I slid my hand into my jeans pocket and pressed Rafael's ring. I hated calling on him, but I didn't have another choice. If I ran, Az would chase me. And he was far faster than me.

"Rafael," I whispered into the night.

Az heard me. His eyes narrowed, and he broke out into a run.

Rafael shimmered before me, took one look at the situation, and poofed me away into darkness. The last thing I heard was Az's roar echoing down the street.

The world shuddered back in around me, though darkness still hugged me close. Something glowed nearby, orange and electric. When I spun to face it, I realized exactly where we were. Rafael had taken me to the goddamn hellgate. It flickered in the depths of the dungeon beneath *Infernal*, heat pouring off Lucifer's seal.

Something about it set my teeth on edge. It felt like death itself.

This wasn't exactly what I'd had in mind.

"Well, I was going to say thanks for saving me back there, but I think I'll pass," I snapped. "Why did you bring me here of all places?"

"You know why." Rafael shoved his hands into his pockets. "You haven't killed Asmodeus yet, and I don't think you're going to manage it. Even with your supernatural soul, you have far too much humanity. You can't bring yourself to do it."

I mean, he was right, but...I hated that it was so

obvious to *everyone* except the one person who needed to see it. Asmodeus himself.

I huffed. "As you could see in the alley, I'm working on it."

"What I saw was a girl who's in way over her head." He rocked back on his heels. "Asmodeus looked like he was two seconds away from ripping *your* heart out. Not the other way around."

"Yeah, well." I sighed. "I'm mortal. He's not. It's not exactly an easy thing for me to do."

"So, what are you saying? You want me to take you back to Hell?" He arched a brow. "Because it sounds like you've given up, which means your soul belongs to someone else. Is that what you want? Because the gate's right there."

"I'm not giving up. It's just taking a little longer than I expected. Besides." I cocked my head. "I thought you *wanted* me to get his heart."

"You're right. I do," he said. "I'd love to see the soul game stop. This world is a nice one. I'd like to stay here. But it sounds like you don't want to do the job. So, I'm trying to remind you what will happen if you fail."

Interesting. So, Rafael wanted to say here, but he didn't seem all that concerned about me losing my soul. Which meant...he probably didn't know the full truth behind Lucifer's motivation. I wondered how he'd feel if he found out.

Of course, he was an actual sociopath so I couldn't begin to understand him.

"If you don't want this world to end, what was the whole point of your murder spree?" I asked. "You killed all those supernaturals for trying to help Az save souls.

Why would you do that if you weren't trying to help Lucifer win?"

"I was just following orders," he said with a shrug. "The Creator is far ahead right now, and Az keeps making it worse. Heaven is a hellscape of ice and cold. I'd rather not go back to that place, to be perfectly honest. There's a reason I left. If I need to kill a few supernaturals, it's worth it."

My heart pounded my ribs. "The Creator isn't ahead, Rafael. Lucifer is."

He barked out a laugh. "Who told you that?"

"Everyone. Asmodeus, the Legion. Gabe and Suriel, your fellow fallen angels. All of them seemed pretty certain about it. They've seen the actual count."

"They could be mistaken." He scowled. "Or they were just messing with you. They don't want Lucifer to win, so who knows what they're willing to say to stop him? The thing is, Lucifer is *behind*. It will take him ages to ever catch up. If he catches up."

"The angels don't lie."

His eyes narrowed. "I see what you're doing. You're trying to turn me against Lucifer so that I won't take you through the hellgate when you fail. Well, it's not going to work, Mia McNally. I have a loyalty to my king, and your soul is his, whether you like it or not."

"Sure." A beat passed. "And then Hell automatically wins. Just how you want it."

"What do you mean Hell automatically wins?" He shook his head and stepped back. "Maybe I shouldn't have come to your rescue after all. Because I don't like the way you're speaking to me."

"What, with the truth?" I followed him with two steps of my own. "I'm an archangel. At least, that's what my soul is. And it's immortal because of a deal my past self made with the Creator. If Lucifer gets my soul, he wins. Game's done. Hell for everyone. It probably doesn't even matter if he's ahead or behind right now. He wins regardless. I know you like this world, but hey. Your side wins. Aren't you happy about that?"

I was laying it on a bit thick, but it was working. Rafael's face had begun to pale.

"I didn't know you had an immortal archangel soul," he said quietly.

"Yeah, neither did anyone else, including me."

"When did you find out?"

"Oh, about twenty-four hours ago." I laughed when his jaw dropped. "Surprised? Yeah, me too. The thing is, Lucifer fed me a lot of lies when he took me to Hell, and I fell for all of them. But he's not trying to save the world, Rafael. He's trying to end it. With a win of his own. And if he gets my soul, it's all over."

The hellgate flared in the dark, the orange light flickering across Rafael's pinched face. I didn't like the guy. He was a murderous asshole. But he was clearly as unnerved by this whole thing as I was. The enemy of my enemy was my friend. At least for now.

"There's a prophecy," he whispered. "That you and Asmodeus will be the end of this world."

"I don't think that's true," I countered. "Has anyone heard that prophecy, other than Lucifer?"

"Yes. *I've* heard it," he whispered with wide eyes. "When Lucifer did. I thought it meant something else, but..." He shook his head. "Over the years, Lucifer kept repeating something slightly different than what I'd heard, and I started to think I remembered it wrong. It's been so long. I even forgot about the original words. Until now."

My heart stilled. "What did you think you heard, Rafael?"

He lifted his gaze to meet mine. "That you and Asmodeus would be the ones to end the *game*. Not the world."

"Oh." My entire body went tense. All this time, I'd thought the prophecy was just another lie, but Rafael had heard it, too.

But could it really be true? Could I have that much power?

"Dammit, Mia," he muttered, jamming his fingers into his hair. "You're the enemy. I'm supposed to take your soul to Hell."

"That's not really what you want to do though, is it?"

With a growl, Rafael grabbed my elbow and blinked me away. When we appeared out of the shadows, we were on small side street somewhere in the city, though I couldn't tell where. It looked like any other street on any other block in any neighborhood. Hopefully, it was far away from Hell's Kitchen. Otherwise, Az would find me.

Rafael pulled a card out of his wallet and pressed it into my hands. A credit card.

I furrowed my brows. "What the hell is this for?"

"You don't have anywhere you can go right now, do you?" he asked.

"Well, I was going to stay at Gabe's, but I guess that's not safe anymore. Az could easily find me there...but I need to catch up with the fallen angels regardless. They'll be somewhere downtown looking for me."

Hopefully, Az hadn't found them.

"You need to stay out of sight. Plus, you need some sleep. Human body, remember?" He nodded and stepped back. "Get a room in this hotel for the night. The card isn't traceable to me. Then, figure out a way to sort this out. You can find the angels in the morning."

"Why are you doing all this?" I asked him. "Two seconds ago, you were ready to drag me into Hell."

"That was before I understood what that really meant." He took another step back, vanishing into the shadows. "I love this world as much as you do. Fix it."

And then he was gone.

Sucking in a breath, I spun on my feet to eye up the grungy hotel. At least it would have a bed and zero demons. Truth be told, I was exhausted. It felt like my skin had been worn down to the bone, and my eyes were so heavy, I swore I was experiencing REM even though I was awake.

I wanted to keep going full send until I found a way to fix this, but that was impossible. I needed a full night's sleep, a shower, and a fresh head in the morning. If I went searching for the angels tonight, there was no telling how long it would take. Az was probably still hunting me. I'd be more likely to get caught than anything else.

Tomorrow night, we'd trap Az. I would take the heart to Lucifer. And all of this would finally be over.

Probably.

As crazy as the plan was, it almost sounded too easy.

L ight streamed in from the open window,
blasting my face like a fireball. Heart in my
throat, I leapt out of bed and crouched like a
crafty ninja. That was when I saw the flowery
bedspread, the warped wooden floors, and the
mismatched curtains I'd forgotten to shut the night
before.

A breath of relief whooshed out of me, and I sagged
against the bed.

I'd forgotten where I was. Alone in a strange bed in a
grungy hotel over in Brooklyn. I'd only figured out my
location when I'd climbed the six flights of stairs to my
rented room and stared out the window at the
Manhattan cityscape in the distance. Rafael had been
smart. Az probably wouldn't venture out of Manhattan
to search for me, and the weird teleporting thing Rafael
did meant he would have lost my scent.

But it also meant I had a long day ahead of me. I
needed to find the fallen angels and the trunk, and then

set up a meeting with Lucifer to make the trade. The heart in exchange for my freedom.

The end of the game, once and for all.

I showered and had a bowl of cereal from the buffet downstairs before pushing out into the streets. One long subway ride later, and I was back in downtown New York. I stayed clear of the streets of Hell's Kitchen and made my way back to the angels' apartment. If they were smart, they wouldn't have come back here. Az and the Legion knew exactly where they lived.

I slipped into the shadows on the opposite side of the street and crouched behind a dumpster. The scent of rotten fish swirled into my nose as I peered around the green monstrosity. There was no movement in the windows. Not a single light was on. Obviously, I didn't have enhanced senses, so I couldn't hear anything other than the frequent taxi horns nearby.

It didn't look like the angels were home. But appearances can be deceiving.

I knew they'd found somewhere else to hide Morax's heart, but they might pop back here throughout the day to see if I came looking for them. They would have found me missing when they'd returned to the alley last night, and I had no doubt they'd searched for me.

Hopefully, they hadn't run into a very angry Legion of demons.

"Thank god you're here." Suriel dropped down in front of me and joined me behind the dumpster. "I didn't get a single wink of sleep last night. We thought Asmodeus had found you."

"He did find me, but I managed to get away," I whispered back, though I didn't know why. It wasn't like anyone would be able to hear me over the sounds of the city. "But I couldn't go back there after. It was too risky."

He patted me on the head and smiled. "Good girl. You're spunkier than I thought you were. How'd you manage it?"

"Er." I might as well come clean. Secrets were tearing me apart. "Rafael."

"Wonderful," he said dryly. "That's just what I wanted to hear."

"He gave me a way to contact him if I got into trouble." I shrugged. "Thought I would cash in on that. His teleporting trick came in handy."

"You do remember what Rafael has done, Mia. Right?" he asked in a dark voice. "He's a killer at heart."

"Trust me. I could never forget. And if we get through this alive, he'll have to answer for his crimes." I said that like it was up to me or something. Like I was some kind of judge and executioner, ready to dole out punishments for murder. But my words seemed to make Suriel happy.

"Alright, let's get out of here. The demons were here scouting the street this morning. I wouldn't be surprised if they came back."

"Which ones?" I asked.

"Phenex," he said. "And Bael."

"Not Caim? Not Stolas?" And definitely not Valac. I hoped he was okay.

Had he managed to use the witch's spell to restore his memories? Had he been able to convince the others to do the same? I was desperate to find out, but I couldn't risk running into them in case they hadn't.

"How did they look?" I asked.

"Pretty much like you'd expect." His lips set into a

229

grim line. "Ready to absolutely annihilate anyone who stood in their way."

My stomach dropped. "So, not ready to make up, then?"

Suriel gave me a sad smile. "I'm afraid not, Mia."

Without another word, Suriel gathered me into his arms and flew me over the top of the buildings to a street several blocks over. He took me to the docks, where warehouses replaced the residential buildings. The last time I'd been in this area, I'd come face to face with Rafael. He'd lured me into one of the warehouses to kill me.

It was funny how things had changed.

We climbed in through a broken window in one of the warehouses. Inside, dust swirled through the empty space. My boots echoed against the concrete as we found a flight of stairs and pushed onward to the next floor.

"Kind of creepy." My voice was loud in silence. "How'd you find this place?"

"We came straight to the docks after leaving you in the alley. Thought we might be able to find a warehouse currently unoccupied. Lucked out with this one. We've been watching the trunk in shifts while searching for you."

Guilt flickered to life. "You weren't searching all night, were you?"

He cast me a sideways glance as we climbed the concrete stairs. "Course we were. We had no idea what had happened to you, and a part of me was scared we'd find you dead in an alley somewhere."

Well, shit. While they'd been worried for my life, I'd been sound asleep in a Brooklyn bed. To be honest, I hadn't realized they actually cared that much. I was just another mortal to them. Or so I'd thought.

"I'm really sorry." We reached the top of the stairs where another empty room spread out all around us. Gabe sat in the very center, leaning against a massive concrete beam. His eyes were practically glued shut. "I thought it was best if I stayed out of sight."

"It was the smart thing to do." He smirked when he saw Gabe asleep. Chuckling, he tipped back his head and shouted, "Danger!"

Gabe leapt to his feet with wild eyes, fisted hands windmilling. When he saw who it was, he dropped his hands and scowled. "I could kill you for that. You nearly gave me a heart attack."

"Serves you right," Suriel said, striding over to him. "I could have been Asmodeus."

"If you were him, me being awake wouldn't stop him from ripping me limb from limb. Glad to see you're alive, Mia. Thought he might have gotten to you." Gabe brushed the dust from his jeans. "He's pissed as hell we took Morax's heart. To be honest, I feel kind of bad about it."

"I know what we need to do," I suddenly said.

The angels both turned toward me with raised brows.

"This is how we're going to trap him." I motioned at the trunk. "You can lure him in with that. He'll go after Morax's heart."

"Yeah, it's a good plan," Gabe said with a frown. "But how exactly will we keep him from murdering us when he finds out the heart isn't in the trunk anymore? I think you underestimate how mad he'll be."

"That's what the *trap* is for, Gabe," I replied. "You

231

have to make sure he gets stuck somewhere he can't get out of."

"And meanwhile, you'll have the heart," Suriel said. "You'll show it to Lucifer, he'll end the game, and then we'll make sure Asmodeus gets his memories back so that he doesn't kill us all when we let him out of his cage."

"Yes," I said with an eager nod. "Simple, right?"

"Very simple," Gabe said with a roll of his eyes. "Nothing could possibly go wrong. Guaranteed success, I tell you. All we have to do is trap a powerful demon, trick another one, and make sure five others don't find out what we're up to."

"Easy peasy." I grinned.

Suriel chuckled. "I don't think that means what you think it means."

"Confidence, guys." I patted both of their shoulders as we formed a circle around the trunk. "Envision success. Let's go save the world."

❀

Suriel, Gabe, and I went our separate ways. They would lure Az into a trap while I did the exchange with Lucifer by the hellgate. I'd called upon Rafael again. He'd set up my meeting with the King of Hell, excited that it looked like we'd win.

I stood by the flickering hellgate with palms as wet as an ocean. This whole thing had been my idea, and I suddenly wasn't so sure I'd made the right choice. What would happen if the angels weren't able to trap Az? Would I be able to get Lucifer to end the game before he found out that he was still alive? This whole thing hinged on him believing the heart belonged to Az.

The King of Hell stepped through the hellgate. His flaming seal flickered around him, transforming his face into a thing of pure evil. As I looked into his eyes, I didn't know how I'd ever believed a word he'd said. Everything about him screamed death and rage.

He wanted to win, and he'd destroy everyone who got in his way.

"I was starting to think you would renege on our deal," he said with a slow smile. "Rafael and Eisheth have been filling me in on your activities. It seems you've been spending a great deal of time with the demon you came here to kill."

"I had to get him to trust me," I said, cursing myself when my voice came out a little wobbly. "He needed to let down his guard around me. I don't know if you noticed, but I don't have supernatural strength. It's not like I could just run at him and attack."

His gaze latched on the object in my hands. I avoided looking at it myself. The whole thing made me queasy. Even when the angels had opened the trunk, I'd only taken a small peek. That was all I could manage. It was a living, thumping heart. It even smelled fresh.

So gross.

"Well, it seems I was wrong to doubt you." He nodded at the object. "Is that the heart?"

"Here," I said, handing him the gift-wrapped package. Suriel had even put a little red bow on it. A bit much, if you asked me, but if it made Lucifer happy, then I'd add a hundred bows myself.

Anything to get this over with.

He took the package and shook it. I winced. This

whole thing was gross. I was standing in the middle of a freaking hellgate dungeon, handing an old heart to a demon. How had my life turned into this?

"How did you manage to do it?"

I swallowed hard. Suriel had expected him to ask something like this, so we'd gone over my story in great detail. We'd come up with the only believable thing. I'd killed Az in his sleep.

"I got him to take me to bed." Annoyingly, my face flushed. "When he fell asleep, I..."

"The old seduction trick." His eyes flickered with what I swore was irritation. It probably was. Lucifer hadn't actually wanted me to do this. He'd wanted me to lose. By giving him Az's heart, he couldn't take my soul. "I must admit, I've underestimated you."

"So, it's all over then, right?" I dared to ask. "I keep my soul, and you'll end the game."

For a moment, he did nothing but stare at me. The light flickered across his face, drowning half of his expression in shadows. His body trembled with barely-contained rage, but there was nothing he could do about my win. He had the heart. He had to give up the game. Those were the terms of our deal, whether he liked it or not.

"You do realize that I can't take your word for what it is," he finally said. "I need to see the heart myself."

My gut clenched. "Is that really necessary?"

"Yes." His brow arched. "Is that a problem?"

"Kind of. It's a *heart*. I never want to see it again."

"And yet you managed to find the courage to rip it out," he said with a smirk.

I pressed my lips together. "Fine. Open the package

and check. If that's what it takes to get this over with, then just do it."

With a whisper of a smile, Lucifer unwrapped the package. I jerked my chin away and stared at the hell-gate. It burned my eyes, but I'd rather that than look at a thumping demon heart again.

He stared down at the heart for so long that it felt like my feet had permanently morphed into the ground. What the hell was taking so long? It was a heart. Massive and red with black veins running through it. Clearly demon. I'd been able to tell that myself, and it wasn't like I was some kind of expert on a demon's cardiovascular system.

"Interesting." He snapped the gift shut. "I didn't think you had it in you."

Of course he didn't. I held back the urge to say exactly what was on my mind, but I needed to play along until the very second he ended the game. Then, I could give him a right piece of my mind. I couldn't wait.

"Your fault for underestimating me," I said.

"Oh yes, I certainly did underestimate you." A wicked smile lit up his face. "It never even occurred to me that you'd be bold enough to deliver me a fake heart."

My stomach dropped to my feet with a splat. I pressed my palms against my jeans to hold my hands steady.

"That's right." He tossed the gift to the ground. "That is not Asmodeus's heart. Did you really think I wouldn't be able to recognize the heart of one of my own Princes?"

"I mean...it's just a heart. A demon heart. Maybe you're mistaken."

"That is *Morax*," he growled. "I have no idea how you got your hands on his heart, but I'd know it anywhere. You've tried to trick me, Mia McNally. Do you know what I do to those who cross me?"

I had a pretty good idea, and it started with a T and ended in Orture.

"Maybe we just need to call a time out for a moment and take a few deep breaths." I took several slow steps away from him. "You're jumping to conclusions, and that's not helpful for anyone."

"I have a better idea. I'm going to make you pay for this."

29

My heart banged against my ribs. Trembling, I started to back away from Lucifer. I could make a run for it. He came in through the hellgate, and I'd left the door leading into the club unlocked. If I went full send, there was a chance I could get away.

"Don't even try it, Mia," he said with a snarl. "This dungeon is a tomb. You won't be leaving unless I allow it."

Maybe I could call on Rafael...although he might not be willing to betray Lucifer right to his face. He'd helped me once, but...he was the kind of person who always looked after Number One. Himself.

"Listen." I held up my hands. "Let's not do anything hasty. If you kill this body, you know I'll just come back again. You were right about my past self's deal with the Creator. He made me immortal."

He rolled his eyes. "I'm not going to kill you, Mia. I made that mistake once. I won't make it again. Your death does nothing to help me."

"Okay." I took another step back. If I couldn't get out of here, I would go down fighting. I wouldn't let him scare me into submission. "So, now what? Shouldn't you let me go? Because from where I'm standing, I haven't broken the terms of our deal. It hasn't been a full week yet. I still have a few days to bring you what you want."

He smiled. "I amend the terms of our deal."

I stopped short. "Amend it? Can you even do that?"

His laughter echoed off the stone walls. "I'm the King of Hell, Mia. I can do anything I want."

"There are rules," I said, my shoulders trembling. "That's the whole point of contracts. They have terms that are clearly laid out when each party signs it. You can't just swap things out when you want."

"You now have twenty-four hours to deliver me Az's heart." He grabbed my arm and shook me until my teeth clattered together. "His actual heart. Not some decoy. Twenty-four hours. And then the deal is done."

"I feel like that's not legally binding. We signed a deal for a week. I still have three days left."

"That was before you tried to trick me." His laughter scraped against my eardrums. "Rendering your contract terms moot. I can now change the deadline to whenever I want. Or did you not read all the clauses?"

Uh oh. I had not read all of the clauses. There had been two hundred and five of them. Who the hell had time for that?

His smile grew wide when he saw the look on my face. "I didn't think you would. Humans. You're so easy to manipulate."

Anger boiled in my veins. Curling my hands, I hauled back a fist to slam it into his face. He caught my arm before it got anywhere near him, and he easily shoved me back. I stumbled over my feet and fell right on my ass.

"So disappointing," he said with a sigh. "Once, you were strong enough to put up a fight. Now, you're like a little bug I could squash at any moment. Boring."

"I know you lied to me." I pushed up from the ground, ignoring his words. I was stronger than he thought I was, and I wouldn't give him the satisfaction of seeing me afraid. "All that stuff you said about the end of the world? You didn't mean a damn word of it."

His eyes flicked across my face, and he smiled. "You got your memories back."

"More than that," I said. "I understand why you were so eager to have me sign your contract. This isn't about Az's heart. It never was. You want my soul. My *archangel* soul."

He lifted his hands and gave me a slow clap. "Well done, Mia. Is that what you want to hear? Because it doesn't matter if you know the truth or not. For you, it changes nothing. You want to keep me from winning the game? You know what you have to do."

"You tried to trap me in an impossible situation."

"I didn't *try*, Mia." He smiled. "From where I'm standing, that's exactly what I've done. Instead of doing what you need to do in order to save the world, you came up with a convoluted plot to steal another demon's heart."

"I hate you," I hissed. "How can you be so focused on this stupid game? Do you want to watch this world implode? Don't you care at all? Can't you see what will happen to this place?"

"Why would I care?" he asked, still smiling. "I'm the King of Hell, destined to rule over my lands for eternity.

These lands make a nice addition to what I already have. And the mortals?" He shrugged. "Maybe if I had a soul myself, then I could find a way to care. Thankfully, I'm not cursed with that."

"You don't have a soul?" No wonder he was the way he was. No one without a soul could have a conscience or empathy for anyone else.

"No." He knelt and collected Morax's heart. I reached out to grab it back, but he held it out of my reach. "I think I'll hold on to this for now."

"Give it back," I said. "It's not the one you want."

"No, but it could come in handy one day." Lucifer stepped toward the hellgate, and the flames roared across his skin. "Rafael will be here in a moment to collect you. And then you'll meet me here tomorrow at midnight. If you come without Az's heart, it will be time to collect your soul. See you soon, Mia McNally."

Lucifer vanished into the hellgate, leaving me alone with empty hands and a hollow heart. I should have known I'd never trick him. But how was I suppose to know he could recognize an individual demon's heart?

Letting out a frustrated roar, I paced the dungeon, trying to come up with an answer to this complicated puzzle. He'd moved up the deadline, and he'd left me without any other options. It was either Az's heart, or it was the end of the world.

30

Rafael shimmered in before me. He took one look at my face and sighed.

"What's happened?" he asked. "I thought you'd figured this whole thing out."

"I brought him Morax's heart." I slumped against the slick stone wall and dropped my head into my hands. "I thought I could trick him, but...I thought wrong."

"Let me guess," he said dryly. "Lucifer wasn't very happy about it."

I snorted. "Understatement of the century. If he wasn't intent on getting my soul, he probably would have killed me right then and there. And now, he's moved up the deadline for our deal."

"To?"

"Tomorrow at midnight." I sighed and glanced up to meet Rafael's dark gaze. "If I don't bring him Az's actual heart tomorrow night, we're all doomed."

"Well." Rafael folded his arms. "I think you know what that means, don't you."

Not a question. A statement. One I refused to hear.

"I'm not doing it," I said softly. "I won't hurt Az."

"So, you'll just let the world end."

Pain flared in my heart, so hot it almost brought me to my knees. This whole thing was far more than I could take, and it had been hammering at me for weeks now. Eventually, I would break.

Just not yet.

I wouldn't give up until the flames stormed across the city streets.

"I don't know, Rafael. Okay?" My eyes swam with unshed tears. Any minute now, and they'd turn into a waterfall down my face. "Just...go ahead and take me out of here."

But he still stood there, hands slung into his jean pockets. "I can see this is difficult for you. A mortal girl holding on to an angel soul. It's tearing you apart."

I shook my head. "It's not my soul that's tearing me apart. It's everything else. I don't want to be the one who decides that this is the end. I didn't even know about any of this until a few months ago. Life was easy, even though I thought it was hard. This whole thing..."

"I understand," Rafael said in a quiet, dangerous voice. "You're not a killer. You're not built that way. But I am. I can help you with this, Mia. Do you a favor. Plunge the knife into his chest so that you don't have to."

"Wait, what?" I jerked up my head, blood rushing out of my face. "No, that's not what I was trying to say."

"Don't you get it?" He strode toward me with flashing eyes. "You're never going to be able to destroy him yourself. You need someone to do the job for you. Once he's taken down, you must be the one to take out his heart. But Lucifer never clarified about the rest of it."

My heart thundered in my chest. "Rafael, no. Please. You don't want to do this."

He searched my eyes like he didn't quite believe my words. "Surely you'd rather this than the alternative. We can do what needs to be done, and you don't have to take part in the worst of it."

"No one is destroying Az. Not me. Not you. Not even Lucifer himself. Okay?" I stalked toward him and shoved my finger into his chest. "Look, I know you're a murderous psychopath or whatever, but you need to back the hell off. I'm going to deal with this. Somehow. I just...need some time to think. Okay?"

He patted me on the head. Like I was some kind of child throwing a tantrum. "You need some time to process this. I get it. You never really considered his destruction as an option, and now you have to. The thing is, Mia. You don't have a lot of extra hours to work through it. You're going to have to face this. Sooner rather than later."

"Are you going to take me out of here or not?" I growled.

He cocked his head, as if considering, and I realized he might actually decide to leave me here. Rafael wanted the world to stay as it was, and he was all too willing to do whatever had to be done. No matter the cost. He might decide that having me out of the way was the easiest option.

"Rafael," I warned.

"Alright," he said with a sigh. "I'll take you out of here. But you need to keep an open mind."

"I'll do whatever I damn well please," I snapped.

"If midnight comes, and you haven't destroyed him? I will." He grabbed my arm and shadowed me out of the dungeon. The world went dark, and a hollow emptiness surrounded me. It stretched on for miles, and something about it clawed at my skin. It was like the darkness wanted to burrow inside of me and never leave. It would become me, and I would become it.

Nothing would ever exist but the void.

My boots thundered onto hardwood, and I crumbled to my knees. As I glanced around, I saw the hotel room I'd stayed in the night before. Suriel and Gabe were both on the bed, their heads wrapped in stained bandages. Blood oozed through the material like a creepy Rorschach.

I gasped and rushed over to the bed. "What the hell happened to them?"

"Guess," Rafael said, folding his arms.

My stomach dropped out. "Trapping Az..."

"It didn't go so well," Rafael finished. "After you told me what you were up to, I swung by to check on them and found them like this. He left them unconscious and bleeding on the floor. They're still in one piece, of course. He didn't try to destroy them. But he made sure to make a point."

"Shit." I pressed the back of my hand against Suriel's forehead. It was hot to the touch. "Won't they heal themselves?"

"Yeah, they'll be fine," Rafael said. "Give them a few hours, and they'll be brand new."

I pushed away from the bed and spun toward him. "Az did this to them. He must be pretty pissed off."

"They stole Morax's heart and then tried to trap him. To be honest, Mia. I'm shocked he didn't do anything worse than this." He shook his head and stepped back.

"I should be going now. Lucifer might call on me, and I don't want to give him any reason to doubt me."

"And you're going to give me until tonight, right?" I asked, my heart skipping a beat.

"I'll give you until tonight." He nodded. "But that's it. Just before midnight, I'll make my move."

I frowned. "Rafael…"

"That's the best I can do." The shadows swirled around him. "See you soon, Mia."

Rafael vanished into the darkness, leaving me alone in a room with two half-dead fallen angels. With a roar of frustration, I returned to the bed to check on their wounds. They'd been knocked pretty hard in the heads, and there were some deep slashes along their arms. But no sign of attempted destruction. No one had tried to rip out their hearts.

Az had spared them.

Not that it mattered. It all resulted in the same thing. He was free, and he would hunt us down.

I slid to my knees beside the bed and buried my face in the freshly-washed sheets. Tears poured from my eyes now that I was alone. Now that Lucifer could not see them. Sobs shook my body as it all came crashing down on me.

We'd failed. Our brilliant plan wasn't so brilliant after all. And Lucifer was less than a day away from winning the game of souls. Collapsing against the bed, I gave in to my grief. I clung on to the bedsheets with trembling hands and let the pain consume me. There was nothing I could do anymore, despite what I'd told Rafael.

I was all out of options.

Lucifer was going to win.

"Mia?" Suriel murmured, slurring the word so that I barely recognized it as my name. I leapt from the floor and rushed to his side, ready with a cold wet towel and some painkillers. He cracked open his eyes. Red streaked through the whites.

"Finally." I smiled down at him. "You've been out for hours. I thought I might have to start blaring music to wake you up."

"What the fuck happened?" he muttered.

I let out a long breath. "Turns out it's harder to trap a Prince of Hell than we thought."

He chuckled, and then winced. "I feel like I've been hit by a truck."

"Well, you looked way worse a couple hours ago." I grabbed his hand and gave it a squeeze. "You had some war wounds. They're all healed up now though."

"Why didn't he destroy us?" Gabe asked, prying open his eyes. He didn't look any better than Suriel did, but at least they were finally conscious.

"Honestly?" I asked. "I don't know. I'm just glad he didn't."

"Did it work?" Suriel asked with a little hope in his bloodshot eyes. "Did you give Lucifer the heart?"

The sigh that exploded from my lips shook me to my very bones. Starting from the beginning, I filled them both in on what had gone down in the dungeon. We'd lost. Morax's heart hadn't tricked the King of Hell like we'd hoped. And we had nothing to show for our efforts.

"He really is a bastard." Suriel yanked the bandage off his forehead and tossed it into the trash can. Trembling, he slowly stood from the bed and wobbled over to the window. "Mia, I hate to say it. But Rafael might be right."

I'd braced myself for this. To them, it was the only way forward.

"There has to be another way," I insisted. "We just haven't thought of it yet."

"How, Mia?" Suriel whirled on me with pain in his eyes. "You came up with a good plan. Probably the best one possible, given the circumstances. We gave it a really good try, but look at where it's left us. It might be time to accept that there's no other way. I know it hurts you, and I'm sorry, but..."

I glanced away from him and ground my jaw.

"You have to fulfill your end of the contract," Gabe said. "It's the only way. Your soul is bound to it. You can't beat it."

"Well, then maybe that's it," I whispered. "We've been looking at this the wrong way all this time. Instead of trying to *beat* the contract, what if we convince Lucifer that it's in his best interest to tear it up?"

Gabe gave me a look that I could read all too well. It said, 'Don't be stupid, Mia.'

"Lucifer's never going to forfeit on the contract. Not when he's so close to getting exactly what he wants. Your soul."

"He wants to see the world burn," Suriel added.

"Because the bastard doesn't have a soul himself," I muttered.

"See, you're finally getting it," Gabe said. "No soul. No conscience. No nothing. It's impossible to beat him when—"

"Wait a minute." Heart hammering, I slowly spun to gaze back at where Gabe still huddled beneath the sheets. "Lucifer doesn't have a soul...but he must have had one at some point, right? I saw this spell in the grimoires, something about creating soulless zombie people. Is that what happened to him?"

Gabe pressed his lips together. "No one is quite sure about his origin. It's not something anyone ever talks about. But...sure. That's a possibility. Although I wouldn't call him a zombie."

A strange prickling sensation scurried down the back of my neck. "So, if he once had a soul and it was taken from him, where the hell is it? Because I bet he would feel differently if he had it again."

"Ohhhh," Suriel breathed from behind me. "I see where you're going with this. You want to reunite Lucifer with his soul that he might finally have some empathy for humanity. And then he'll stop the game. Not because of a deal. But because he wants to."

"Yeah," I whispered. "I know it sounds crazy, but..."

"No crazier than anything else," Gabe grunted.

He threw back the sheets and pulled a tee over his

head, joining us by the window. We all stared out at the silent streets below us as our minds spun through the implications. Lucifer was a soulless monster, but...what if he *wasn't* anymore? What if we could make him whole again?

"We've got less than twenty-four hours to figure this out," I finally said. "Any idea where we go from here?"

"Unfortunately, no." Gabe frowned. "His soul could be anywhere. Possibly not even here in the mortal world. It's much more likely to be in the afterlife. And it would be like searching for a needle in a haystack."

"There's no one here we could really ask about it," Suriel continued. "It happened so long ago. Lucifer might be the only one who knows where it is, and I doubt he'd go anywhere near it. He wouldn't want to accidentally reunite with it. A soul is like a magnet. It would find him if he got too close."

My mouth dropped open, and I sucked in a sharp gasp. Realization pounded down on my head, and I had to grasp the windowsill to keep from falling over. "Oh my god. I know where his soul is."

The angels turned to me with matching expressions of awe.

"You do?" Gabe asked. "But how? Where?"

"There's only one place in this world that Lucifer is afraid of. Inexplicably so. A place he avoids at all costs." I nodded, an intense certainty settling in my gut. "It's somewhere in the East River, below the Brooklyn Bridge."

It made so much sense. Lucifer wouldn't step foot on the damn bridge. Why? Because if he did, he'd regain his soul, and the last thing the King of Hell wanted was a conscience. The answer had been there all this time, right below our noses.

If we wanted to end this whole horrible, twisted game, we needed to get Lucifer on that bridge. And it would have to happen tonight.

32

This was it. The last day of the rest of our lives unless I pulled this off. As the New York buildings lit up for the night, I said goodbye to Suriel and Gabe. The fallen angels were going to keep the Legion distracted while I faced Lucifer on the bridge.

Suriel clamped his hand on my shoulder as we stood on the hotel building's rooftop. The wind was in his face, blowing back his golden hair, but he didn't seem to notice. "You sure about this?"

I nodded. "Everything might go horribly wrong, but I have to try. For Az."

Tears welled up in Gabe's eyes, and he gave a little sniffle. "I hope Az someday understands everything you've done for him.

"Me too," I whispered. As it stood, he still didn't remember me. For whatever reason, he'd avoided the restoration spell. There was no guarantee he would ever cast it, even if we won tonight. He'd decided he didn't trust me. I didn't know if he ever would.

It made me feel hollow. Like I'd lost a chunk of myself.

Can't think about that now, Mia. I needed to focus. Even if we managed to trick Lucifer onto the bridge, there was no guarantee it would go the way we needed. At the end of the day, my hunch was just a hunch. I was putting the fate of the entire world in the hands of a hidden soul.

After saying goodbye to Gabe and Suriel, I waited in the hotel for Rafael. Without him, this plan would never work, and I didn't much like depending on a psychopath. Unfortunately, he was my best and only option for getting Lucifer onto that bridge.

He appeared in a storm of shadows, clad in all black. An open takeout box sat in his hands, and he munched on some fries while he gave me a quick scan. "Nice outfit. You look like you're ready to kick some ass."

I'd also donned an all-black outfit. Dark leggings, dark top. Better for blending in.

"I've got a new plan, but I need your help," I said to him as I paced the length of the hotel room.

He leaned against the wall and munched on another handful of fries. "If it's not ripping out Az's heart, then I don't want to hear it."

I tsked, whirling on him. "A shame. Because it's way better than that."

He considered me for a moment, and then he sighed. "I can't believe I'm even entertaining this, but go on. What do you have?"

"If I give him Az's heart, Lucifer ends the game, but you know what I've realized? There's nothing stopping him from starting it up again." I nodded when Rafael's eyes widened. "He agreed to end it, but he never said anything about it being *permanent*. And you know he's a tricky bastard. I wouldn't put it past him."

"Fine," he grunted. "You have a point. But I don't see how there's anything you can do to change that now. You've already signed the damn deal. The terms are set in stone unless you break another clause."

"Or if Lucifer decides to tear it up."

He folded his arms and lifted his brows. "And why would he do that?"

"I'm going to reunite him with his soul, and then he'll never be a problem to this world ever again." A beat passed. "Because he won't want to be."

Rafael let out a low whistle. "Alright, I see where you're going with this. You want to give him a conscience. That could work actually."

"And, lucky for us, I know exactly where his soul is."

"Yeah, me too. He's had me looking for it, to make sure it's still there. It's somewhere in the East River."

So that's what I'd overheard when that Pyro guy had told Lucifer about Rafael's failed search. He must have wanted to confirm it was there so he could continue to avoid it.

"But you didn't find it," I said.

"No, but it's there. I can sense it." He shook his head and tossed a few more fries into his mouth. "Only problem is, Mia, he won't go near that damn bridge. So, if we can't get him near his soul, we have to take it to him. How are we supposed to do that when we can't find it?"

"Why do you think I've asked you to help me?" I arched a brow. "You have a knack of taking people places, even where they don't want to go."

"Oh, I see. My power," he said with a smile. "You actually really do need me, don't you?"

"Don't push your luck," I warned. "I might need your help, but I haven't forgotten what you've done to the supernaturals of this city."

"Well, in that case, maybe I should just let you deal with this whole thing on your own." His gaze shuttered, blocking out his emotions. "I can tell by the look on your face that you'll never forgive me. Hell, I bet you and your little Legion will even put me on trial."

He wasn't wrong about that. Right now, we had bigger fish to fry, but Rafael needed to pay for what he'd done. He had to answer for his crimes. I just didn't think I could be the person to make him do that.

"What if I make you a deal?" I shook my head at my own question. Deals were evil. I hated them. But this one might be the only way to get Rafael to do what I wanted.

"I'm listening." He set down his takeout box and levelled his gaze on my face.

"I won't turn you over to the Legion as long as you don't kill anyone else."

"Interesting. What about the human authorities?" he asked.

"The human authorities wouldn't know what to do with a murderous fallen angel. So, no. I wouldn't hand you over to them either."

"Alright," he said. "Agreed. You going to make me sign a contract?"

"No. I don't like contracts. As long as you play your part, then I'll keep up my end of the bargain."

Smiling, he leaned forward. "So, what exactly do you need me to do?"

❀

A light wind whipped off the bridge, tugging my hair away from my face. I pulled the air into my lungs and relished in the scent of this city. New York might not be perfect, but it was mine. Vibrant and loud. Full of so much life. And this was only a small pocket of the world. So many cities and towns and villages were scattered across this big, beautiful planet.

All of it would be gone if I didn't stop Lucifer.

The wood creaked beneath my boots as I strode over the first hump in the bridge. I would wait in the very middle where the beams rose up high in the sky. It was the best way to ensure Lucifer's soul would find his body.

Just as I reached the designated spot, an uneasy tremor shot down my spine. Someone was here, watching me from the shadows. I gulped and fisted my hands, wishing I had something to protect myself with.

That was when I saw him.

Az stood on the far end of the bridge, backlit by the city lights. Shadows whipped around him like a storm cloud, and the fire in his eyes shot through me even from afar.

No. I shook my head. He shouldn't be here. If Lucifer saw Az before I reunited him with his soul, it could ruin everything.

"Stay where are you, Az," I called out to him.

Obviously, he didn't want to listen to a damn word I said. He stalked down the bridge, shoving past a few tourists taking a midnight stroll. It was like he'd barely even noticed they were there, his eyes too locked on my face.

Fear throttled my heart. Should I run? He'd just follow me if I did. Here I was, a sitting duck, and there was nothing I could do about it. If I called Rafael, it would take him away from the hellgate. Right when he needed to be there. It would sabotage everything.

Az slowed to a stop a few feet away from me. Abaddon hung in one hand while his other formed a fist. With a shaky breath, I searched his eyes. There was nothing familiar in the pure hatred I saw in them.

"Hi," I whispered. "You really shouldn't be here."

"Why?" he growled out. "Don't want me to witness you meeting with another enemy?" When I opened my mouth to speak, he cut me off. "I know about Rafael, Mia. I saw him blink you away with my own two eyes. You and he are as thick as thieves. Hell, I wouldn't be surprised if you've helped him kill."

"Now, that's not fair," I said. "He helped me get away from *you*. For safety. That's hardly the same thing as murder."

"It is where he's concerned." His grip on the pommel tightened. "Where's Morax?"

My blood burned through my veins. "I don't know."

Narrowing his eyes, he stalked closer. "Tell me where he is. I know you're the one who took him. You and all your fallen angel friends. Funny, isn't it? You all leave your homeland behind and then clump together here like a ball of mud."

"A ball of mud? Wow."

"Where's Morax?"

"I honestly don't know. But if I were to guess, he's probably in Hell."

His eyes flashed with rage. "Well, then you're going to go to Hell and get him back for me."

Okay, so this was at least somewhat promising. It meant he didn't plan to shove Abaddon into my heart anytime soon. But I still needed to get him off this bridge. When Lucifer realized I'd tricked him, I had a feeling he would lash out. He wouldn't take it out on *me* though. He still needed my soul. So, what was the best option after that? He'd target the person I loved most in the world, to drive the knife in deep.

"Okay." I nodded. "I'll find Morax for you."

He blinked, like he was taken aback. I guess he thought I'd argue with him. "Now."

"Now is not exactly a good time. In fact, it's probably best for you to go home and—"

"More excuses," he murmured. "More lies."

"I wish they were," I whispered. "But you need to go home now. I don't want you to be here when..."

"When what?" he asked.

"I can't tell you that."

If I did, he'd insist on staying. He'd give the game away. I'd probably have five seconds where Lucifer thought I was waiting here to hand him the heart before he realized what I'd done. But I needed that five seconds. Hopefully, it would be long enough for his soul to find him.

If he saw Az before that five seconds was up, he'd spot the trap for what it was.

He shook his head, grinding his teeth together. "I don't know what it is about you, but you're the most frustrating woman I've ever met. You and those damn fallen angels. The world would be better off if I could bring myself to get rid of all of you, but I can't."

For a moment, my heart nearly stopped. He couldn't bring himself to destroy us. Did that mean he could sense the truth, deep down inside of him? Did he recognize me even if his conscious thoughts didn't make the connection?

"Because you're the only ones who know where Morax is," he finished.

Oh. My shoulders sagged. Of course that was it and nothing else. How could he recognize me if the image of me was gone from his head?

"So, this is it," he said with a nod. "You're going to give me Morax's heart."

"I told you," I said, throwing up my hands. "I don't know where it is."

"Then, start looking!" His voice boomed like thunder. Fisting my hands, I tried to come up with a way to talk him off this ledge, but I knew it would be impossible. Stubborn Az. He'd never give up. He was desperate to find Morax, and I couldn't blame him, especially when I could see the torment raging in his eyes.

Something shimmered on my left. With a gasp, I whipped sideways toward a bundle of shadows forming into the shape of two men. My heart banged my ribs. Lucifer was here, and Az was just there. Right in the line of sight.

"You need to go," I said in a panicked voice, rushing to block him from view. But he pushed me to the side, storming toward the shadows.

"No! Get back!" I screamed.

But it was too late. Lucifer was already here.

33

Lucifer blinked in before me. His lips curled when he spotted Az, and a wicked laugh exploded from his throat. Clearly, he thought he'd won. We'd brought him here to fight.

But then his gaze swept across the beams stretching up into the night sky. His smile fell. Panic flickered across his face, and an animalistic howl sent shivers of unease rippling down my back.

"What have you done?" he asked, stumbling back. "Why have you brought me here?"

"I think you know why," I said flatly, folding my arms. "Didn't you lose something around here, Lucifer? Wouldn't you like it back?"

"Rafael?" Lucifer whirled on the fallen angel, who had stumbled far out of his path. "Take me out of here. You don't know what you've done."

"Actually." Rafael shrugged. "I know *exactly* what I've done. Enjoy your new life."

Rafael vanished into the night just as a light rain fell

from the rolling clouds. Thunder cracked through the night.

"Get out of my way." Az shoved me aside and stormed toward Lucifer with Abaddon held high. He threw his sword toward the King of Hell's throat. I screamed and rushed at him, grabbing his arm.

His aim hurtled to the left, missing Lucifer's skin by a sliver of an inch.

He shook me off and whirled to glare at me. "I swear to god, Mia. Don't make me turn my sword on you next."

"Listen to me, Az. You don't want to destroy him. That means the Creator wins and—"

"It's better than the alternative," he said in a grim voice.

"No, it's not." I grabbed at his hands, but he'd already turned away. He threw his weight behind another blow, but we didn't have the element of surprise on our side anymore. Lucifer was ready. He pulled a dagger from his waistband, ducked beneath the sword, and slashed at Az's shirt.

"Get away from me!" Lucifer shouted. "Stay back or I'll destroy you both."

Az growled.

Lucifer dodged back and flared his wings. The black melted into the night.

"No," I gasped, shaking my head. He couldn't fly out of here. Not yet. He didn't have his soul back. If he got away, we'd never be able to get him out here again, and midnight would pass with no end to the game.

I'd forfeit my soul.

He would win.

"Stop him," I screamed at Az.

He whirled toward me with a glare. "I thought you didn't want me to fight him!"

I grabbed his shirt and begged him with my eyes. "He has to stay on this bridge. His soul is hidden some-where in the East River, and it has to reunite with him. If he gets away, that will never happen."

Az probably wouldn't believe me. So far, he'd rebuked me no matter what I said. To him, I was the enemy. And for good reason. Without his memories, all he could see was terrible things.

But he nodded, spread his wings, and pushed off the ground. The demons danced in the air above the bridge. Az swooped in, and Lucifer darted back. It was a storm of feathers and rage. With a roar, Az rushed him. Lucifer grabbed Az's arm and threw him away with all his might.

Az hurtled through the air, vanishing into nothing more than a ball of light.

My stomach dropped.

Oh shit.

Lucifer laughed and sneered down at me, his wings beating hot air on my face. "Nice try, but you've lost, Mia McNally. Five minutes to midnight. Your time is up, and Az is gone. I cannot wait to watch you burn for eternity."

Blinking back tears, I gazed off in the distance, fear coiling around my heart. What had he done to Az? Would he make it back? Or would the world end before I had the chance to see his face again?

Lucifer turned to go. I screamed up at him, my face drenched in rain and sweat. There was nothing I could do. Damn mortal body. I needed wings. I needed to fly. The only way to stop him was to throw him back down here and force him to face the soul he'd left behind.

Az rushed in from the dark clouds, storming straight toward Lucifer's back. He slammed his body into his. Thunder and lightning cracked through sky, so loud I fell to my knees. A white hot explosion almost blinded my eyes. Their wings drooped. And then they fell.

The two demons collapsed in a heap in the middle of the Brooklyn Bridge. A few human tourists screamed and ran, but not before taking a few photos with their phones. I scurried over to them both with tears staining my cheeks.

I knew Az could survive any fight, but I'd never seen anything like that in my life. Two immovable forces slamming together, almost cracking the world in two.

A strange ripple rushed across the bridge and set my teeth on edge. I stiffened and glanced up, half-expecting to see an army of demons charging toward us. Hell had arrived. It was all over. The flames would consume us now.

But nothing was there. The world continued to tick by, normal and quiet and eerily calm. Like two demons hadn't just battled each other in the midnight sky.

Lucifer cracked open his eyes and groaned. I jumped to my feet and stumbled back. I didn't want to be within arm's reach if he decided he needed to throttle someone.

I'd been the cause of all this. It would probably be me.

"I should really hate you for this, Mia McNally," he choked out.

"Okay..." I watched him warily as he rolled to the side and clambered to his feet. "Are you saying you *don't* hate me for this?"

"A part of me does." He brushed off his pants. There were several rips in them from the force of the collision. "But that part is hidden now. Thanks to you."

"Wait a minute." My heart flipped. "Are you saying it worked?"

"You restored my soul," he said, his voice still rough. "I've been avoiding it for centuries. Funny how a mortal girl was the one who finally bested the demon. I suppose the prophecy came true in the end."

"And the world?" I glanced around.

"I forfeited the game," he said. "Two seconds before midnight. And don't worry. I forfeited the contract, too. Your soul is safe. At least from me."

I almost fell to my knees in relief. It was impossible. So impossible I felt kind of numb. We'd actually...won. The world wasn't going to end. Az's heart was safe and so was my soul. I could have screamed for joy if it wasn't for Lucifer's weirdly chilled expression.

"This is weird," I said, narrowing my eyes. "You sound so normal. So not...demony."

He still looked the same though. That bright silver hair. Those cutting ears and sharp jawline. The elaborate tattoo swirling across his neck. Large and muscular and impossibly powerful. He might have his soul now, but he was still very much a demon.

"I'm far more in control of my demonic urges in this form." He tugged at his shirt, frowning at the wrinkles. "To you, that might make me seem normal."

"And you're not angry?" I asked. "A few seconds ago, you didn't seem too keen on me restoring your soul."

He sighed. "The demon in me is angry, but he's not

in control anymore. So, no. I'm not angry. My life tends to be more difficult like this, but I'm not angry."

"Okay..."

"Asmodeus will be waking up soon."

As if on cue, Az flipped open his eyes. His gaze locked on mine, and his breath hitched. A single finger lifted from his side and reached toward me.

"Mia?" he whispered. "Is that you?"

Heart in my throat, I leapt into his arms.

"Mia," he murmured into my hair. His arms were strong and steady around me. His lips pressed against my cheek, and he breathed me in. I'd never been happier in my life. He was back. Asmodeus was back. My heart was so full it wanted to burst right out of my chest.

"You actually remember me," I whispered, pulling back to search his face. "You know who I am and everything that's happened."

Jaw clenched, he nodded. "I can't believe he made me forget you."

At that, we both turned to Lucifer who was watching the reunion with a vacant expression on his face. He might have his soul back, but he clearly wasn't a mortal being. Whatever empathy he'd gained, it was deep below the surface.

"You," Az growled.

"Don't be angry, Asmodeus," Lucifer said lightly. "It wasn't my fault. The Creator removed my soul, and terror reigned. At least it's all over now. And don't worry. I'll return Morax's heart to you."

"The Creator did this?" I asked.

"Of course he did." Lucifer frowned. "Who else would have done it?"

"My memories are back. How did you do that?" Az asked.

Lucifer blinked at us blankly. "I'm the King of Hell."

I rolled my eyes. "That's your answer for everything."

"Of course it is." He sighed. "Now, is there anything else?"

"What do you mean?" Az asked with narrowed eyes.

"I'd really like to get going now. As nice as this world is, it's not my home. And New York is far too noisy for me. All that technology buzzing away. I don't know how it doesn't drive all of you crazy." He cocked his head. "I don't know. Maybe it does. Humans are very strange creatures who do inexplicable things. Perhaps it has something to do with all that buzzing electricity you surround yourselves with. Allyria is so nice and quiet. It's like a tomb."

I gaped at him. That was quite the speech.

"Are you honestly just going to fly out of here like nothing has happened? After everything that you've done? All the pain and heartache you've caused?"

"I don't know what else you want from me, Mia. I ended the soul game. The world is safe. Your boyfriend's memories are back, and you have your soul. You're all set for a very long time. And I would like to return to Allyria."

Az pushed up from the ground, still reeling from the

fight. "If you have your soul, why do you want to return to Hell?"

Lucifer shrugged. "I imagine it's the same reason you want to stay here, despite all of Manhattan's disadvantages. It's your home. You belong here. And I belong in Hell. It's all I've ever known."

"So, you're just going to return to the flames and rule over all the torturous demons and crazy hellbeasts. Even though you have a soul now," I said flatly.

"I've done it before." He shrugged. "And I'll do it again. Now, excuse me, I'd like to reach the hellgate before morning."

Lucifer stepped around us and strode down the bridge, head held high, shoulders thrown back. He looked like anyone else out for a late stroll. Except for the massive body and bright silver hair, but who was counting?

We watched him until he vanished out of sight.

Az let out a low whistle. "I can't believe it's over."

"My plan actually worked," I whispered, tipping back my head to gaze up at him. "And it had an unexpected development. A very positive one. You got your memories back."

A lazy smile spread across his face, and his hand trailed down to my hips. "I remember everything."

A little tickle between my thighs brought a gasp to my lips. A part of me couldn't help but fear all of this was another one of Lucifer's tricks. It seemed too good to be true. We'd won. In every way imaginable. The monster had been defeated, and the lovers were reunited. Everyone was safe.

Az palmed my cheek with his other hand. "You look scared."

I leaned against him and breathed in the scent of fire. "It's been a very long time since something went right. I'm afraid that if I trust this, it will vanish into mist. A formless thing that doesn't exist."

He leaned down and brushed his lips against mine. "If you're imagining it, then we're sharing the same dream. And if that's all it is, then I'm happy to be stuck in it forever."

I sighed, lacing my hands around his neck. "I missed you so much, even when you were here. I thought I'd never find you again."

He brushed a stray tear from my cheek, deepening the kiss. Our lips crashed together. Hunger tore through me. I needed this so much that I couldn't hold back the tears any longer.

Az pulled away and clutched me against his chest, letting me sob into his chest. He held me like that for ages, and every emotion I'd bottled up came crashing into him. When my tears had finally dried, Az pulled back and pressed his forehead against mine.

His gaze pierced me. "There's something I need to say to you. I didn't say it before because I thought it was too much too soon, but I won't make that same mistake again. Even though I'm immortal, there's no guarantee of tomorrow." He sucked in a deep breath. "I love you, Mia McNally. *This* you. The mortal girl with fiery hair, a fierce smile, and endless courage. I want you by my side. Always."

My heart lifted in my chest, and I clung tightly to his neck. "I love you, too, Asmodeus, the First Prince of Hell and Commander of the First Legion. And I'm glad you want me by your side because you're going to have a hell of a time getting rid of me. I'm here to stay."

Our lips locked, and an inexplicable *zing* went through my gut. A new one. One far different than I'd ever felt before. It was as if we'd started again. A fresh love. A fresh life. And no one could ever take it away from us.

Not even the King of Hell.

EPILOGUE

"Good morning," I called out as I bustled into the kitchen with Hendrix perched on my shoulder. Apparently, it was one of his new favorite things to do. Fine by me. I liked his company.

Az stood at the stove, flipping pancakes. My stomach growled as I perched on the stool and watched him work. The muscles in his back rippled as he moved, highlighted by the overhead light hanging from the lofted ceiling.

I felt happy, calm, and content.

And all because I'd fallen in love with a demon.

He spooned the pancakes onto a plate and delivered them to me on the kitchen island. Immediately, I dove in, moaning at the fluffy goodness. Az really knew how to make the best pancakes in all of New York City.

Hell, maybe even the entire world. A world that was not going to end in an icy wasteland *or* a flaming hellscape. Pretty awesome, right?

"The Legion want to meet us at the club in a bit," he said with a smile. "Even though the world is safe from

Lucifer, there's still things to do and killers to track down. Is that alright? Or would you rather...?"

"Spend the rest of the day in your bed?" I grinned around a mouthful of pancakes. "The latter would be preferable, but I know we can't turn our back on the city now. Besides, we've got the rest of our lives to spend together."

Az strode over to me and slung an arm around my shoulder. His kiss was fierce and electric, curling my toes. "Yes, Mia. We certainly do."

❀

*W*hen we walked into the meeting room, the Legion leapt out from the corners and flipped on the lights. Their shouts knocked me back, and my hand flew to my heart. Hundreds of balloons were crammed into the small space, and the folding table hid beneath a massive array of cakes, cookies, and chips.

"What the hell is this?" I laughed when they finally quietened down. Pri and the rest of the dancers stood off the side, and Serena launched herself into my arms. I couldn't help the massive grin on my face. Everyone was here.

"We wanted to throw you a party," Phenex grunted from the corner. Ever since we'd restored the Legion's memories, he'd been sulking around like a grump. "You know, because you saved the world and all that."

I arched my brows and cupped my hand behind my ear. "What was that? Did I hear you say something nice about me?"

He grunted again. "I'm sorry, alright? I was really shitty to you, and I shouldn't have been."

My heart ballooned. "You didn't know me, Phenex. I can hardly blame you for reacting the way you did. I probably would have, too. But...thanks. I appreciate the apology. And in case you're wondering, I very much forgive you."

Unshed tears swelled in his eyes, and he blinked them away. Caim laughed and slung his arm around my neck. "You got to the big guy. I've never seen him like this."

"Shut it, Caim." Phenex pounded his fist against his palm. "Keep it up, and *I'll* get to *you*."

I grinned. Things were starting to feel like they were normal again. Or as normal as anything could be in a world with demons, fae, vampires, and wolves. And me. A human with an archangel soul, who had fallen in love with the First Prince of Hell.

That kind of normal. The only one I wanted.

We dug into the cake and the chips. Laughter boomed all around me, and the buzz of conversation filled my soul with hope. We were all going to get through this. Together. Lucifer had followed through with his promise. He'd given back Morax's heart. Valac and I already had a few leads in tracking down the rest of him. We were going to bring the Legion back together again, no matter how long it took.

As the party died down and the dancers slowly went home, I found myself settling in beside the metal folding table and letting the day's celebration relax the knots in my shoulders. Priyanka said goodbye, and so did Serena. All that was left was me, Az, and the rest of the Legion.

We cleared the table, and Bael brought out the cards. After we played a few hands, Caim cleared his throat and said what we were all thinking but hadn't been brave enough to say ourselves.

"So," he said. "What's next?"

I smiled. I'd been expecting this. "We won. Who's to say anything is next?"

Bael leaned back in his chair until the front legs tipped off the floor. "Lucifer isn't the only asshole in the world."

"He's right." Stolas nodded. "We probably wouldn't even have to look very far to find another one."

All the demons turned to me. Every last one of them. Even Az.

I held up my hands and laughed. "Why are you all looking at me like that?"

"Why do you think?" Az asked softly. "You're the one who saved us, Mia. It's your call."

I arched a brow. "*What's* my call?"

"Don't play coy." Caim grinned. "You know what we're saying."

"You want to know if the Legion should stay in Manhattan and track down supernatural serial killers. Like a detective agency or something. Just like you did before. Only this time, you don't have to hide it from anyone, right? Since Lucifer knows and doesn't care."

"Nah, we'd probably keep it on the down low as much as we could," Stolas said. "You know, for under-cover purposes."

My lips twitched. "Undercover purposes."

"We're demons," Phenex said with a growl. "Got to keep up certain appearances, don't we?"

"Sure," I said. "I just don't know why you're asking *me*. If you want to track down supernatural serial killers, then you should. Someone needs to."

Az rested his hand on my knee, and for a moment, the rest of the world fell away. "You've been through so much the past few months, Mia. If you want things to be happy, easy, and fun, no one would blame you. And I'll be there right by your side. Whatever you decide, it's you and me, alright? If you want a peaceful life, then I'll happily give you that."

I beamed at him, grinning ear to ear. It was me and him against the world. But the world needed us.

"Besides," Caim said. "We only want to do this if you're a part of it."

I dragged my gaze away from Az to scan the faces of the Legion. Each one gave me a nod in turn, a silent recognition that I was one of them now. They wouldn't do this unless I was with them.

"Let's hunt down some killers." I smiled at the Legion. "One fight at a time."

ACKNOWLEDGMENTS

This book would not be what it is without the help of my husband. Thank you for talking me through the plot and keeping me going with coffee, pep talks, and dark chocolate bars.

Thank you to my Patreon subscribers, Tiffany, Jennifer, and Amy. Your support means the world. I also want to thank all my early readers and members of my Facebook group. You guys are the best!

ALSO BY JENNA WOLFHART

Demons After Dark: Covenant

(Paranormal Romance)

Devilish Deal

Infernal Games

Wicked Oath

The Fallen Fae

(Epic Fantasy Romance, completed series)

Court of Ruins

Kingdom in Exile

Keeper of Storms

Tower of Thorns

Realm of Ashes

Prince of Shadows (A Novella)

The Paranormal PI Files

(Urban Fantasy/Paranormal Romance, completed series)

Live Fae or Die Trying

Dead Fae Walking

Bad Fae Rising

One Fae in the Grave

Innocent Until Proven Fae

All's Fae in Love and War

The Supernatural Spy Files

(Paranormal Romance, completed series)

Confessions of a Dangerous Fae

Confessions of a Wicked Fae

The Bone Coven Chronicles

(Urban Fantasy, completed series)

Witch's Curse

Witch's Storm

Witch's Blade

Witch's Fury

Protectors of Magic

(Reverse Harem, completed series)

Wings of Stone

Carved in Stone

Bound by Stone

Shadows of Stone

Otherworld Academy

(Reverse Harem)

A Dance with Darkness

A Song of Shadows

A Touch of Starlight

A Cage of Moonlight

A Heart of Midnight

ABOUT THE AUTHOR

Jenna Wolfhart spends her days tucked away in her writing shed. When she's not writing, she loves to deadlift, rewatch Game of Thrones, and drink copious amounts of coffee.

Born and raised in America, Jenna now lives in England with her husband, her two dogs, and her mischief of rats.

www.jennawolfhart.com
jenna@jennawolfhart.com

Made in the USA
Middletown, DE
09 May 2022

65524308R00170